R8
10/19

W9-DBN-658

GUNFIRE ECHOED
INTO THE LOBBY . . .

Longarm dashed through the lobby toward the stairs, bounding past guests who stood in shocked immobility. He took the stairs three at a time, his long legs carrying him up to the second floor quickly and easily.

His Colt was in his hand when he reached the landing. His free hand caught the stair railing and swung him around in a tight turn. Another shot slammed closer this time. Longarm caught a whiff of burned gunpowder in the air.

As he looked down the corridor, a man came hurrying around a corner. Longarm spotted a gun in the stranger's hand. The man paused and whipped around to snap another shot behind him, down the cross hall. Then he whirled toward Longarm.

"Hold it!" Longarm called as he leveled his Colt. . . .

TABOR EVANS

LONGARM

AND THE
PISTOLERO PRINCESS

JOVE BOOKS, NEW YORK

This is a work of fiction. Names, characters, places, and incidents are either the product of the author's imagination or are used fictitiously, and any resemblance to actual persons, living or dead, business establishments, events, or locales is entirely coincidental.

LONGARM AND THE PISTOLERO PRINCESS

A Jove Book / published by arrangement with
the author

PRINTING HISTORY
Jove edition / May 2000

All rights reserved.
Copyright © 2000 by Penguin Putnam Inc.
This book may not be reproduced in whole or in part,
by mimeograph or any other means, without permission.
For information address: The Berkley Publishing Group,
a division of Penguin Putnam Inc.,
375 Hudson Street, New York, New York 10014.

The Penguin Putnam Inc. World Wide Web site address is
http://www.penguinputnam.com

ISBN: 0-515-12808-2

A JOVE BOOK®
Jove Books are published by The Berkley Publishing Group,
a division of Penguin Putnam Inc.,
375 Hudson Street, New York, New York 10014.
JOVE and the "J" design
are trademarks belonging to Penguin Putnam Inc.

PRINTED IN THE UNITED STATES OF AMERICA

10 9 8 7 6 5 4 3 2 1

LONGARM

AND THE
PISTOLERO PRINCESS

Chapter 1

Through slightly bleary eyes, Longarm studied the woman who stood in the hotel corridor in front of his open door. His insinuating gaze ran over her, taking in all the details from the shiny toes of her polished, high-buttoned shoes to the curling blue plume of the hat perched atop a mass of ash-blonde curls. In between, the woman wore a conservative dark blue gown that failed to completely conceal the intriguing curves of her body.

"Well," said Longarm, "you don't look like any soiled dove I ever saw before."

The woman's blue eyes widened a little in surprise. "Why would you think I'm a . . . a trollop?"

"Because the bellman downstairs was bound and determined that I was going to get laid tonight," Longarm explained, "even though I told him all I wanted to take upstairs was this bottle of Tom Moore he rustled up for me."

The big federal lawman held up the bottle of Maryland rye he was clutching in his left hand. "Rather cozy up to it than some whore . . . beggin' your pardon, ma'am."

He never would have spoken so crudely to a woman— unless she wanted him to—had he not been tired, frustrated, and a little bit drunk. His boss back in Denver, Chief

Marshal Billy Vail, had sent him here to Kansas City on what Longarm considered to be a piss-poor job, not at all the sort of thing to which he was accustomed. Still, Longarm obeyed orders when it was at all possible and not too damned inconvenient, so he had delivered his prisoner just like Billy said, and now he was ready to get back to Denver on a train that was leaving the next morning.

At the moment, however, he had another predicament. He frowned and said to the blonde woman, "Are you going to get in trouble with your pimp if you don't come back with the money?" He didn't want to cause a problem for the woman, but he'd be damned if he was going to pay for it, either. This was certainly a dilemma.

The woman took a deep breath, which lifted the small but pert breasts under her dress. She appeared to be trying to keep from losing her temper as she said tightly, "You *are* Deputy Marshal Custis Long?"

Longarm nodded. "That's me, I reckon."

"My name is Katherine Nash. I work for the Bureau of Indian Affairs."

Longarm's frown deepened. He raised his right hand and scraped his thumbnail along the line of his jaw as he thought about what she'd just told him. Finally he said, "Then you're not a whore?"

Katherine Nash rolled her eyes, then said in a voice dripping with scorn, "You're drunk, Marshal. Perhaps I made a mistake by coming to see you."

Longarm reached over and with a thump set the bottle of Tom Moore on a chest of drawers just inside the hotel room. He gave a little shake of his head. "I'm sorry, ma'am. To tell the truth, I reckon I *am* a mite under the influence. But it's nothing a cup or two of black coffee won't fix. The dining room downstairs is probably still open. Can I meet you there in, say, five minutes?"

Katherine Nash hesitated before replying, then shrugged and said, "I suppose so. I was told by my superiors that you're one of the most efficient federal officers. I'll give you a chance to prove that to me, Marshal Long. But only *one* chance."

"Yes'm," Longarm said, bobbing his head in a nod. "I'll be right down."

Katherine Nash started to turn away. She said coolly over her shoulder, "I'll be waiting . . . for five minutes."

Longarm closed the hotel room door, drew in a couple of deep breaths, and scrubbed his hand over his face, feeling the beard stubble. If he hurried, he just might have time to scrape the stubble off before he went downstairs . . .

He caught a glimpse of himself in a mirror as he passed through the hotel lobby on his way to the dining room. His appearance had improved a considerable amount in a very short time, he thought. He'd shaved, washed his face, retied the knot in his string tie, and slipped back into the jacket of his brown tweed suit. His longhorn mustache was curled properly on the ends, and his snuff-brown Stetson sat squarely on his head. He was the very picture of a modern federal marshal, he thought.

Of course, it had taken him a shade over five minutes to accomplish that. He hoped Katherine Nash of the Bureau of Indian Affairs was still waiting for him.

Longarm stepped into the arched entrance of the dining room and took off his hat as he looked around. The place wasn't busy, since it was fairly late in the evening. Longarm had no trouble spotting the plume on Katherine Nash's hat. She was sitting at a table across the room.

He went over to join her and saw that there was already a pot of coffee and a cup and saucer on the table. As Longarm pulled back a chair, Katherine said, "I took the liberty of ordering that coffee you said you wanted. I was afraid it would take more than a couple of cups, however, so I told the waiter to leave the pot."

"Much obliged," Longarm said. "I'm feeling a lot better already."

As a matter of fact, that was true. Knowing that he had made a fool of himself in front of a BIA agent—and a

3

damn pretty one at that—had gone a long way toward sobering him up. He poured himself a cup of coffee anyway and sipped from it. Black as midnight and strong enough to walk off by itself. Just the way he liked it. The only thing that would have improved the coffee was a dollop of Maryland rye . . . but then, that would have been sort of defeating the purpose, wouldn't it? he asked himself.

"You don't want any coffee?" he asked Katherine Nash.

She shook her head. "It keeps me awake, and I have to get my beauty sleep."

A smile tugged at Longarm's mouth. Katherine was the stiff sort, and that comment about getting her beauty sleep was the first hint that she might unbend a little under the right circumstances. He sipped from the cup again and said, "So, you work for the BIA."

"That's right. Does that surprise you?"

"No, ma'am." Female employees of the federal government were rare, but somewhat less so in the Bureau of Indian Affairs. In the course of his career, Longarm had met several female BIA agents. Of course, most of them hadn't been as pretty as Katherine Nash.

"I feel that it's my duty to do what I can to help our poor, oppressed red brothers and sisters."

Longarm managed to nod without cracking a smile or making some reference to Mister Lo. Chances were, Katherine wouldn't understand, and if she did, she would probably be offended. Anyway, it wasn't as if Longarm didn't feel both respect and sympathy for many of the tribesmen, even those he'd clashed with over the years. He just didn't like the way a bunch of do-gooding, bleeding-heart bureaucrats from back East thought they had all the answers to all the problems without ever having walked a mile in the moccasins of the Indians or the boots of the white settlers.

"I suppose you've got some official business with me?" he asked.

Katherine Nash nodded. "My supervisor wired Chief Marshal Vail in Denver requesting assistance, and he was

4

kind enough to inform us that you were already here in Kansas City. Delivering a prisoner, I believe he said?"

Longarm nodded curtly and didn't say anything. He didn't want to think too much about Rollie Ashdown.

When Longarm didn't comment, Katherine went on, "We—and by that I mean the Bureau of Indian Affairs—would like for you to investigate a certain situation for us."

"Trouble?" murmured Longarm.

"Perhaps. That's what we want you to find out and prevent if at all possible." Katherine picked up her bag, opened it, and took out a piece of thick paper that had been folded several times. She unfolded it, smoothed it out on the table, and turned it so that Longarm could read the gaudy printing on it. "Have you ever seen one of these?"

Longarm grunted. He wasn't sure what he had been expecting, but what he saw on the paper wasn't it.

The paper was an advertising flier for Colonel Jasper Pettigrew's Wild West Show and Frontier Extravaganza. That much was written in fancy curlicue script at the top of the page. Below that legend was described in somewhat smaller letters the series of attractions offered by the show: trick riding by the lovely Miss Jessamine Langley; appearances by the famous scout, Indian fighter, and buffalo hunter Asa Wilburn; amazing displays of shooting skill by the beautiful Princess Little Feather of the Pawnee; and a grand finale consisting of an exhibition battle between a troop of United States cavalry and a band of fierce, bloodthirsty Indian savages. The flier was illustrated by several crude but colorful drawings.

Longarm said, "What the hell's a Wild West Show?"

"It's a new sort of attraction recently begun by Colonel William F. Cody," Katherine explained. "The performances by Colonel Cody's troupe have been so popular back East that similar shows have been formed, including this one."

"Bill Cody always was as much of a showman as anything else," mused Longarm. He tapped the advertising flier with a long, blunt index finger. "I never heard of this fella Pettigrew, though."

"He claims to have been a colonel in the army during the Indian Wars, but I've checked with the War Department and they have no record of his military service. I suspect he's simply a charlatan and a promoter."

"No law against that," Longarm said with a chuckle and a shake of his head.

"No, of course not. But there are other aspects of this matter that concern the Bureau."

Longarm studied the flier. "This so-called battle between the cavalry and the Indians?"

"No, that's just acting," Katherine replied offhandedly. She pointed at another line on the paper. "It's this right here."

"Princess Little Feather?" Longarm asked with a frown. "I reckon it's a mite odd they're using an Indian gal as a sharpshooter, but I don't suppose there's anything illegal about it."

"There is if she's being held against her will," Katherine said grimly.

Longarm leaned forward. He had downed only about half of the cup of coffee, but he didn't really need any more. He was stone-cold sober now. "You're saying she's been kidnapped and held prisoner?"

"That's what we would like for you to find out, Marshal."

Longarm shook his head, not in refusal of the assignment but in confusion instead. "What makes you think this Princess Little Feather is being held against her will?"

"We were contacted by our agent on the Pawnee reservation. It seems that one of the chiefs, a man named Lame Bear, somehow came into the possession of one of these fliers, and he saw the picture of Princess Little Feather." Katherine touched the drawing of a young Indian woman dressed in a fringed buckskin dress. The woman in the drawing had a pistol in her hand and was shooting at a target. "Lame Bear claims to recognize the girl as his daughter Sky Song, who disappeared during a battle with the army twelve years ago."

6

Dubiously, Longarm shook his head. "That's just a drawing some artist scribbled on there. You can't tell anything from it."

"Nevertheless, Lame Bear insists that this woman, who is now billed as Princess Little Feather, is really his daughter. He says that she would never stay with the white men of her own free will and allow them to debase her like this for the sake of some performance. He wants her returned to him, or else he will lead the tribe in an uprising."

"Except for a few scrapes, the Pawnee have been pretty peaceful for a while now," Longarm pointed out.

"And the Bureau would like very much to keep it that way."

Longarm thought for a moment, then said, "You know there's a mighty good chance this gal ain't who Lame Bear thinks she is."

Katherine inclined her head in agreement. "Of course. But we still have to investigate and determine that beyond a shadow of a doubt, so that when we report the results of the investigation to Chief Lame Bear, he'll be satisfied."

Longarm grunted. "What makes you think he'll believe you? If he's that convinced the gal's his daughter, he's liable to go on the warpath anyway."

"We have to try to resolve this peacefully," Katherine said earnestly. "And Chief Marshal Vail did say that you were to cooperate with us, Marshal Long."

Longarm fished a cheroot out of his vest pocket and stuck it in his mouth. He didn't ask for Katherine Nash's permission before he snapped a lucifer to life with his thumbnail and held the flame to the end of the cheroot. After he'd shaken the match out and taken a couple of puffs, he asked, "Where is this here Wild West Show?"

Katherine Nash smiled and said, "Serendipity."

"Beg pardon?" Longarm had never heard of a place with that name.

"Colonel Pettigrew's troupe is currently staging performances right here in Kansas City," Katherine said. "They'll be here for several more days before leaving to go to Denver on the next part of their tour."

"They're taking a Wild West Show and going west?" Longarm said with another puzzled frown.

"Their ultimate destination is San Francisco, I understand. The tour began in New York City, with stops in Philadelphia, Washington, Baltimore, Chicago, and St. Louis. Evidently Colonel Pettigrew feels that reversing the normal course of such a troupe will allow him to steal a march on his competition."

"He's got competition? Besides Bill Cody, I mean?"

"So I'm told, though I don't really know anything about that. Nor is it germane to your assignment."

"Well," muttered Longarm, "I sure as hell wouldn't want to do anything that ain't germane."

"Excuse me?"

Longarm shifted the cheroot to the other side of his mouth and reached for the advertising flier. "I said I reckon if Billy Vail and the BIA want me to look into this, I reckon I'll see what I can find out." A thought occurred to him. "If Princess Little Feather really does turn out to be Lame Bear's little girl—and I ain't saying that's likely to happen—what do we do then?"

"Return her to her family and her new home on the reservation, of course."

"What if she don't want to go?"

"I'm afraid she won't have much choice in the matter," Katherine said sternly. "As an Indian, she is a ward of the United States government. We can't allow a war to break out with the Pawnee."

Longarm didn't say anything. He considered the possibility to be so unlikely that it wasn't worth worrying over.

He started to fold up the flier. "Can I have this?"

"Certainly."

"Where do I find these folks?"

"I believe they're staging a performance tonight at the local arena. And the troupe is staying at The Cattlemen's Hotel."

Longarm tucked the flier in an inside pocket of his jacket. "I'll pay them a visit."

"Thank you, Marshal."

"How do I get in touch with you?"

"Why don't I come back here tomorrow night?" Katherine asked.

That struck Longarm as a little strange. He had expected the BIA agent to tell him the name of the hotel where she was staying. But if Katherine Nash wanted to protect her privacy, it was really no business of his. He said, "I'll have to postpone my trip back to Denver. I was supposed to catch a train tomorrow morning."

"There'll be another train, I'm sure. And don't forget, we've already been in touch with Marshal Vail. He knows not to expect you back right away."

Longarm shrugged and then drank the rest of the coffee in his cup. It had grown cool, and it really needed a slug of Tom Moore in it now. He started to get to his feet.

Katherine Nash stopped him by saying, "Thank you, Marshal."

"No thanks necessary," said Longarm. "I'm just doing my job."

"I know you were perhaps expecting some time off, though. It must be quite a strain, having to guard a prisoner night and day, especially one as notorious as Rollie Ashdown."

Longarm grimaced. He had expected a hard job, too, considering Ashdown's rep as a mad-dog killer. The fella had deserted from the army, after all, and murdered three other soldiers in the process. He'd been on the run for weeks before a local lawman in Wyoming had nabbed him trying to steal some food from a store. Then Ashdown had been sent to Denver for safekeeping until the army decided what it wanted to do with him.

That decision had put Longarm on a train with Ashdown, and they had ridden across eastern Colorado and all of Kansas until they crossed the Missouri River and reached Kansas City, Missouri, where they'd been met by a whole

9

squad of army guards from Fort Leavenworth who would escort Ashdown back to Washington, D.C. That was where his court-martial would be held, and that was where he'd be hanged when the trial was over. The army couldn't allow a soldier to kill three of his fellow soldiers and get away with it.

Even when he was just a sad, confused little gent who'd been jumped by three non-coms who intended to beat him to death with their bare hands because they were drunk as skunks and had decided they didn't like the unlucky private's looks. It had been a sheer fluke—aided no doubt by the drunken state of the non-coms—that had allowed Rollie Ashdown to get his hands on a pistol and defend himself. But the only witness had seen Ashdown come running out of an alley with a smoking gun in his hand, leaving the three corpses behind, and that would be enough to convict him.

At least, that was the story that Ashdown had told Longarm during the tedious hours on the train, and the words had had a ring of truth about them. Longarm had encountered his share of brutal sergeants during his own term of military service in the Late Unpleasantness. He knew that Ashdown might be telling the straight story, for all the good it would do him.

But Longarm had turned the little fella over to the guard detail anyway. There wasn't a damned thing he could do otherwise. And there was always the possibility that Ashdown had been lying through his teeth and really was a cold-blooded killer. Scant comfort, that, but at least it was something.

Still, the whole job had left a bitter taste in Longarm's mouth, and he'd been trying to wash it out with Maryland rye when someone had knocked on the door of his hotel room and he had opened it to find Miss Katherine Nash standing there. It was *Miss* Nash, wasn't it? he thought.

Longarm realized he didn't know. He ignored Katherine's comment about Rollie Ashdown and said, "You ain't

10

married, are you?" He didn't see any rings on her long, slim fingers.

Katherine looked a little surprised by the question. "Why, no, I'm not."

"Want a family someday?"

"Well . . . of course. I suppose so. But right now, I've dedicated my life to doing everything I can to relieve the plight of those less fortunate."

The answer didn't surprise Longarm a bit. He smiled faintly and said, "You can't save the world, you know."

"Perhaps not." Katherine's voice grew stronger as she went on, "But one can try, can't one?"

Longarm came to his feet and nodded. "One can," he said. He tugged on the brim of his hat and turned to walk out of the dining room, hoping that this job would turn out better than the last one he'd been handed.

Chapter 2

Well, it sure as hell *sounded* like there was a war going on in there, Longarm thought as he paused on the sidewalk just outside the entrance of the large arena at the Missouri State Fairgrounds. The huge building would have taken up a couple of city blocks, had it not been in the middle of several acres of show barns, exhibit halls, and animal pens. Longarm took a last puff on his cheroot, dropped it in the dirt, and ground out the butt with his boot heel.

Guns continued to pop inside the arena. The sounds of battle meant that the Wild West Show was staging its grand finale, the mock fight between Cavalry troopers and Indians. Longarm was pretty certain the U.S. Army hadn't loaned Colonel Jasper Pettigrew any real soldiers, so the bluecoats were likely out-of-work cowhands or aspiring actors. He'd have to take a look at the Indians to determine whether or not they were real.

He walked up a slight incline toward a ticket booth. A tall, broad-shouldered, balding man stood beside the booth. He held up a hand as Longarm approached. "Show's just about over, cowboy," he said. "Come back tomorrow night and I'll be glad to sell you a ticket."

Longarm wondered for a second how the man could tell that he'd done some cowboying when he was dressed in a suit, the way Lemonade Lucy, President Hayes's wife, wanted all federal employees to be. He put that question out of his mind and nodded toward the arena entrance. "Need to go on inside anyway," he said.

"Nope, not tonight." A hint of impatience entered the man's voice. "I told you, the show's almost over. Now move along."

Longarm started to reach inside his coat.

The ticket seller's hand darted into the booth and came back out holding a sawed-off shotgun. He pointed the weapon at Longarm and growled, "Try to pull a knife or a gun on me, mister, and I'll blow you in half."

Longarm stood absolutely still for a moment. He'd had scatterguns pointed at him before, but that didn't mean he liked the crawling sensation that went up his back as he looked at the twin dark holes of the shotgun's muzzles. When he trusted himself to speak calmly, he said, "I was reaching for my identification, old son. Now, why don't you put that sawed-off greener down before I take it away from you and shove it up your ass?"

Loud cheering and applause erupted from inside the arena.

"Identification?" the ticket seller repeated. Then understanding dawned on him. "Oh, hell. You're a lawman." The muzzles of the shotgun drooped toward the ground.

"That's right," said Longarm. "All right if I finish what I started?"

"Yeah, go ahead," the man said resignedly. Clearly, he thought he was in trouble.

Longarm took out the small leather folder that contained his badge and identification papers. In the light that came down the incline from inside the arena, he showed the bonafides to the man and then put them away.

"Federal man, eh? I figured you for a local badge."

"Nope."

"The local boys must have called you in, then."

"Now, why would they do that?" Longarm asked, curious.

The ticket seller frowned. "Because of all the trouble we've been having. Hell, the Colonel's yelled about it to the law loud enough and long enough. I thought everybody knew about it."

Longarm shook his head. "Not me. I'm here to see Colonel Pettigrew about something else."

"I was hoping maybe you could get to the bottom of it." The burly ticket seller looked disappointed. He put the greener back in the booth and waved Longarm on toward the entrance with his other hand. "Show's almost over. You ought to be able to catch the Colonel before he goes to his dressing room if you'll wait just behind the gates on the other side of the arena."

"Much obliged," Longarm said with a nod. He strode on inside.

The arena consisted of a large, dirt-floored oval surrounded by tiers of grandstand seats that rose for several levels. Each section had red, white, and blue bunting hung on the front of it, making the place look sort of like a political rally was being held. Longarm walked all the way to the end of the inclined walkway so that he could look around. Every seat in the place seemed to be filled. Men, women, and children whooped and hollered and clapped in appreciation of the epic struggle that was going on in the center of the arena.

A thin haze of dust hung in the air, kicked up by the hooves of the horses milling around. "Soldiers" in blue uniforms, being led by a portly man in a buckskin jacket and a huge white Stetson, exchanged gunfire with a motley band of Indians in breechclouts, leggings, beaded vests, and feathered headdresses. Longarm squinted as he looked at the Indians. Normally he could identify the tribe a warrior belonged to by the markings on his face and the decorations he wore. These "savages", however, were wearing a hodgepodge of ornamentation that might have looked good to the paying customers but really didn't have any more significance than a hill of beans. The insignia sported by the soldiers on their uniforms were all wrong, too, although

14

Longarm supposed they would look real enough to anybody who didn't know any better.

A lot of the Indians had already "died" in the battle, and more of them did so as Longarm watched. They pitched dramatically off their mounts and fell sprawling in the dust of the arena. They would have to be careful not to get stepped on by any of the riderless horses, but that was probably the only real danger they faced.

The walkway ran to both right and left, curving around the oval in front of the grandstands. Longarm spotted the gates in the wall that surrounded the arena. It would be closer to head to the right, so that was what he did.

He kept watching the mock battle from the corner of his eye as he walked around the arena. If this was the sort of thing that Bill Cody was doing these days, Longarm was willing to bet that old Buffalo Bill put on a better show. For all of his braggadocio and grandiose notions, Cody knew the Plains Indians about as well as any white man could, and he was very familiar with the army as well. He would at least try to get things right, Longarm thought.

The phony soldiers swung down from their horses and formed a phalanx as the Indians launched their final charge. The man in the fringed coat and white Stetson stood in the very front, blazing away at the galloping Indians with a pistol and looking noble and fearless. Each of the Indians in turn met his predestined end, plunging to the floor of the arena in supposed death, until only one warrior was left. He drew back the lance in his hand, ready to cast it at the man in the white hat, who had to be Colonel Jasper Pettigrew. The colonel fired just as the Indian threw the lance. The weapon arched through the air and landed point first in the ground about ten feet in front of Pettigrew. It quivered from the force of the impact. Meanwhile, the warrior who had thrown the lance had fallen off his horse, the last of the red men to bite the dust.

Longarm grunted and shook his head in bemused contempt. The rest of the crowd, however, was eating up the ham-handed melodramatics.

Longarm went down a short set of steps that put him on the same level as the floor of the arena. The same dirt was underneath his boots as he walked over to the large double gates. The horses would be led out through here and back to their corrals when the show was over, he supposed.

Several men in range clothes were waiting behind the gates. One of them spotted Longarm and came over toward him. "Something I can do for you, mister?" he asked.

The man was tall and rawboned, with sandy-brown hair under a thumbed-back, sweat-stained hat. He wasn't wearing a gun, Longarm noted.

"Fella outside told me I might could catch Colonel Pettigrew here when the show's over. I'm a lawman."

The man's eyebrows lifted. "Damn well about time somebody did something about that son of a bitch," he said as he stuck his hand out to Longarm. "Name's Ben Price. I'm the head wrangler for the show."

Longarm shook Ben Price's hand and asked, "What son of a bitch? You don't mean Colonel Pettigrew, do you?"

"Hell, no! I was talking about Cherokee Hank, of course." Price frowned. "Aren't you here about the trouble we've been havin'?"

The wrangler had made the same mistake as the man at the ticket booth. Longarm had never heard of anybody called Cherokee Hank, had no idea what connection the man might have with Colonel Pettigrew's Wild West Show, and didn't really care. He said, "I'm here to talk to the colonel about something else."

"Damnation!" Price exclaimed. "I thought the law was finally going to do something. Guess I should have known better," he added bitterly.

Longarm couldn't help it. All this talk about trouble was making him feel mildly curious. That was just the lawman's instincts in him coming out, he supposed. But before he could ask any more questions, one of the other cowboys called, "They're comin' out, Ben!," and Price turned back toward the gates.

A couple of the wranglers swung each gate back and the

horses began milling through the opening, cavalry mounts and the smaller Indian ponies alike. The wranglers caught their reins and began leading them in small groups along the dirt-floored aisle that led back to the corrals. Now that Longarm was getting a closer look at the animals, he concluded that the quality of the show's horseflesh wasn't much better than its historical accuracy or its dramatic presentation. This was pretty much a ragtag outfit, he decided.

The supposedly dead Indians had gotten to their feet in the center of the arena, and along with the mock cavalrymen, they were taking bows to the audience. There was still a lot of hooting and applauding going on. The man in the big white hat stepped to the forefront of the group. He had gotten his hands on a megaphone, and now he lifted it to his mouth and said in a booming, gravelly voice, "Thank you for coming tonight, ladies and gentlemen, to witness this dramatic re-creation of the last great Indian battle of the plains! We hope that you have thrilled to this exciting panorama of battle and that you have been educated and entertained! Tell all your friends about Colonel Jasper Pettigrew's Wild West Show and Frontier Extravaganza! We shall be performing here in this magnificent arena for the remainder of the week! Now, thank you—and good night!"

With a flourish, the colonel swept his white hat off his head, waved it in the air, and then bowed low to the applauding crowd. After a moment, the applause died away, and the spectators began making their way toward the exits. Colonel Pettigrew clapped his hat back on his head.

The soldiers and Indians began leaving the arena, following the same path through the big gates as the horses. Standing to one side out of the way, Longarm listened to the snatches of conversation he could hear as the men filed past him. Most of it was good-natured bitching and joshing, and there was some speculation on how big the "house" was, which Longarm took to mean the number of people in the audience. The last man out of the arena was Colonel Pettigrew. Longarm stepped out to intercept him.

"Colonel Jasper Pettigrew?" Longarm asked. He already had his identification ready in his hand.

"Who wants to know?" Pettigrew snapped. Not surprisingly, he wasn't as impressive-looking close up. He was sweating heavily. He reached up and peeled off a false mustache and goatee that Longarm figured were designed to make him look more like Bill Cody. He had a drinker's face, florid and bulbous-nosed.

Longarm held up his bonafides so that Pettigrew could see them and said, "United States Deputy Marshal Custis Long."

Pettigrew's surly attitude changed immediately. He held out a hand and exclaimed, "A federal man! Hell's fire, I never expected Uncle Sam to take an interest in my little bitty ol' problem, but I'm mighty pleased to meet you, Marshal." Pettigrew's speech was more relaxed now that he wasn't performing.

"Just so's you don't get the wrong idea," Longarm said as he shook Pettigrew's hand, "I'm not here about whatever problems you've been having, Colonel. I need to talk to you about another matter."

Pettigrew's face fell. "You didn't come to find out who's been tryin' to run me out o' business? Not that I don't already know. It's that damn-blasted Henry Trenton! I just can't prove it."

Longarm couldn't help but wonder if Henry Trenton was also known as Cherokee Hank. Still, he didn't want Pettigrew getting off the subject, so he said, "Is there some place we can talk in private?"

"Come on back to my dressin' room." Pettigrew jerked a thumb toward an open door that led into a brick-walled corridor. "I could use a snort."

Longarm fell in step beside the showman as they went along the corridor past several open doors leading into large rooms that had been taken over by the troupe and used as dressing rooms. The soldiers and Indians were inside, changing out of their costumes into regular town clothes.

Longarm noticed that one of the Indians had already donned a derby hat and a silk cravat.

"Those Indians of yours look like the real thing," he commented.

"Of course they're the real thing," Colonel Pettigrew said. "I go to great lengths, son, to insure the authenticity of all our performances."

Longarm didn't respond to that, not wanting to get Pettigrew angry with him. Instead, he said, "They're from several different tribes, though, aren't they?"

"Well, sure. It ain't that easy to find Injuns who know anything about the show business. We got mostly Crow and Pawnee, but there's some Sioux and Arapaho and what have you."

"Get along all right, do they?" asked Longarm, thinking about some of the ancient tribal hatreds that had led rival bands to war with each other and enslave each other for centuries.

"Oh, hell, yeah. As long as they get paid on time." Pettigrew chuckled. "Look at it like that, they might as well be white men."

He came to a closed door and opened it, ushering Longarm into a smaller, private room. Pettigrew tossed his hat onto a chair and started removing his buckskin jacket.

"What can I do for you, Marshal?" he asked.

Longarm reached inside his coat and took out the folded advertising flier. He opened it, pointed to the drawing of Princess Little Feather, and said, "It's about her."

"The Princess?" Pettigrew said with a frown. "What about her?"

"I'd like to talk to her, if I could."

Pettigrew turned to a small dressing table. A bottle of whiskey sat on it. He picked up the bottle, pulled the cork with his teeth, and spat it out into his other hand. "Snort?" he asked, holding out the bottle toward Longarm.

"No thanks." Longarm had had more than enough rye earlier in the evening. "What about Princess Little Feather?"

The colonel lifted the bottle to his mouth and took a long swallow, making the whiskey gurgle as the level went down. Longarm wasn't sure if Pettigrew was trying to avoid the questions about Princess Little Feather, or if the man was just badly in need of a drink. When Pettigrew finally lowered the bottle, he wiped the back of his other hand across his mouth and then answered readily enough, "I 'spose she's gone back to the hotel by now. Her act's on earlier in the show, and since she ain't in the finale, there's no reason for her to stay here until it's all over."

Longarm frowned. "You let a young woman walk back to the hotel alone from out here?"

"'Course not," Pettigrew replied, a little indignantly. "We've got a buggy, and one of the wranglers drives her back."

"Ben Price?" Longarm asked on a hunch, though he couldn't have said why.

"Nope. Ben's the head wrangler, so he usually sticks pretty close until the show's over every night. I reckon the boys take turns about drivin' the princess." Pettigrew downed another slug of whiskey, though not as large a swallow this time. "You ain't told me what this is about, Marshal."

Longarm hesitated before answering. If Princess Little Feather really was being held against her will—and as unlikely as that seemed, the fact that she was escorted back to her hotel room every night and maybe even locked in made the likelihood a little more plausible—then Colonel Pettigrew couldn't be expected to admit anything. Longarm said, "I really have to talk to the lady personal-like, Colonel. No offense."

"None taken," Pettigrew said, and he seemed to mean it. "It ain't like I don't have enough problems of my own without mixing in with whatever the federal gov'ment wants with Little Feather." He got a shrewd look on his face and went on, "Say, you don't happen to have any pull with the local law, do you, Marshal? Somebody's been raisin' hell ever since we got to Kansas City—"

Before he could go on, the door of the dressing room opened, and a small, bald-headed man in a dusty black suit bustled in, followed by a tall, lanky, craggy-faced, white-haired individual in buckskins.

"Jasper, I must speak to you—" the bald man began, then stopped short as he noticed Longarm standing there. Quickly, he said, "I am sorry. I did not know you had a guest. I will come back later." He had a European accent of some sort, not thick but definitely there. He began to back toward the door.

The buckskin-clad man stopped him by dropping a heavy hand on his shoulder. "The hell we'll come back later," the man rumbled. "Colonel, Schilling here says he ain't a-gonna pay me tonight."

The bald-headed man snapped over his shoulder, "You can wait until tomorrow, like everyone else."

"That ain't a-gonna do it. I got a lil' gal waitin' for me tonight, and I figure on showin' her a bang-up time."

A flash of recognition went through Longarm's brain. He put it together with a name he had seen earlier without really noting its significance. "Asa Wilburn," he said.

The buckskin-clad frontiersman looked over at Longarm. "Yeah? Do I know you, mister?"

Longarm grinned. "No, but I saw you clean out a saloon once in Abilene. I was there with a bunch that'd just brought a herd up the trail from Texas."

"Lemme guess," Wilburn said. "I busted you one."

"No, sir," Longarm said with a shake of his head. "I wasn't much more'n a younker, but I already had some sense."

Wilburn chuckled. "Must've, to steer clear o' me in those days. Who was I fightin' with, a bunch o' gandy-dancers from the U.P.?"

"That's right."

"Never did get along with that bunch. Shot buffler for 'em all day so's they could eat, and then they always tried to cheat me at cards. Must'a had a hundred or more brawls with them hardheaded Irishers." Wilburn looked Longarm up and down. " 'Pears you could hold your own in a fight. Done some growin' up since them Abilene days, I'll bet."

"Been down the trail a ways, that's for certain sure," Longarm allowed.

The bald-headed man—Schilling, Asa Wilburn had called him—said, "Not to interrupt these rustic witticisms, but I really must get back to work. Jasper, please tell Mr. Wilburn that he will receive his wages tomorrow, the same as everyone else in the troupe."

Pettigrew rubbed his jaw. Silver beard stubble rasped under his fingertips. "Aw, hell, Kurt," he said after a moment. "If Asa's got a gal waitin' for him tonight, I don't 'spose it'd hurt anything to give him a little advance on what he's got comin'."

Schilling rolled his eyes, but he nodded in acceptance of Pettigrew's decision. "You are the boss," he said. "But you are not the most astute businessman in the world, Jasper."

"Never have been," Pettigrew admitted cheerfully. "We'll be all right, though, if that dadblamed Trenton'll just leave us alone."

Wilburn said, "So I get my money?"

Schilling sighed. "Come with me back to the office. I shall give you an advance. A *small* advance."

"Don't be too tightfisted, now," Wilburn was saying as he and Schilling left the dressing room. "You're a Prussian, not a Scotchman, you know."

When they were gone, Pettigrew shook his head. "Sorry about the interruption, Marshal. Now, you were sayin' about Princess Little Feather . . . ?"

Longarm wasn't saying anything about her other than that he wanted to talk to her, but before he could repeat that to Colonel Pettigrew, there was another interruption. Outside in the arena somewhere, a man yelled something incoherent, and the shout was suddenly drowned out by the thunder of galloping hoofbeats.

Longarm stiffened. He had heard the sounds of the fake battle before, but this was nothing like that. Every instinct in his body told him that this was the real thing.

This was trouble.

22

Chapter 3

"What in the bloody blue blazes!" Pettigrew exclaimed as he lunged toward the door, the bottle of whiskey still in his hand.

Longarm was closer. He reached the door first, jerked it open, and stepped out of the dressing room. He looked to the right, toward the direction of the wide, dirt-floored corridor that led from the arena to the corrals. The sound of hooves came from that way, and it was getting louder.

Somewhere in the corridor, a man screamed.

Longarm broke into a run. Men were coming out of the other dressing rooms, and in a matter of seconds, the hallway was clogged with people. Longarm bulled his way through as best he could, saying loudly, "Get out of the way, damn it!"

He saw horses sweep by in the main corridor, galloping wildly from the direction of the corrals toward the arena where the performance had taken place earlier. Longarm shouldered up to the opening, but he was careful not to step out into the path of the stampede.

Colonel Pettigrew's Wild West Show and Frontier Extravaganza used fifty or sixty horses, and Longarm judged that nearly every one of them raced past him, out of control. Their hoofbeats had drowned out the screaming, so that he couldn't tell when it had stopped. But as the horses reached the arena and poured into it through the still-open gates, so that the stampede wore itself out and the noise died down some, Longarm realized that nobody was screaming now.

That struck him as not necessarily a good thing.

He stepped out into the main corridor. Dust hung in the air, and the dirt floor was churned up by the racing hooves. Longarm looked to his left and saw what he had hoped he wouldn't see: what looked like a pile of bloody rags that was really the sprawled body of a man who had been caught in the stampede.

Longarm had seen men trampled by runaway herds of longhorns, chopped up by the hooves of the beasts until they didn't look like anything that had once been human. This wasn't that bad, but it was bad enough. Longarm ran toward the fallen man, aware that Colonel Pettigrew was puffing along right behind him, panting, "Oh, Lord, oh, Lord!"

From the other direction, toward the corrals, several men came running, among them Ben Price. Longarm reached the injured man first, dropped to a knee beside him, and immediately saw that it was no use. The fella was dead, and it had been an ugly death at that. His skull had been caved in by the flailing hooves, and his body was bloody and misshapen. A sour taste in the back of his mouth, Longarm came to his feet and shook his head.

Colonel Pettigrew clutched his arm and said, "Marshal?"

"Nothing we can do for this hombre now, Colonel. Who is he?"

Ben Price and the other wranglers came hurrying up in time to hear Longarm's question. "His name was Alf Culpepper," Price said. "One of our wranglers. He should've been out at the corrals. He shouldn't have even been here." Price added bitterly, "He wouldn't have been if I hadn't sent him back out to look for a saddle somebody lost."

"Dadgum it, Ben, what happened?" Pettigrew demanded. "How'd that stampede start?"

Wearily, Price shook his head. "I don't know. We'd just

started turnin' 'em into the corrals, as usual. They were pretty high-strung, like they always are right after a show. I saw some sort of flash, and all of a sudden they were runnin'. There was no way we could stop 'em, Colonel."

One of the other wranglers spoke up. "I didn't see any flash. What are you talking about, Ben?"

Price turned sharply toward him and snapped, "Are you accusin' me of something, Beaumont?"

The other wrangler was a wiry, compact man with an angular, dark-completed face and thick black hair under his Stetson. He shook his head and said, "I'm not accusing anybody of anything. You're a mite touchy, aren't you, Ben?"

Price looked like he was going to answer hotly once more, but the colonel stepped forward and moved between them. "That's enough, boys," he said. "Alf's dead. Show a little respect."

Clearly, there was bad blood between Ben Price and the wrangler called Beaumont, Longarm thought. But that didn't necessarily have anything to do with the tragic accident that had claimed the life of Alf Culpepper.

Assuming, of course, that the stampede had really been an accident. . . .

A woman's voice, shrill and frightened, suddenly cut through the air. "Ben! Ben, are you all right?"

The crowd that had gathered around the body in the center of the aisle parted and a young woman hurried through the gap. She was wearing some sort of pink wrapper and had long blonde hair that fell in thick waves down her back. She practically threw herself into Ben Price's arms and wound her arms around his neck, hanging on to him tightly as if to convince herself that he was alive.

"Jessamine!" Price exclaimed. "Jessamine, honey, take it easy! I'm fine. It was poor old Alf who got trampled."

The young woman glanced toward the body, then shuddered and buried her face against Price's chest, rubbing her cheek against his shirt. "Oh, how awful!" she gasped.

"What happened? I was in my dressing room, and I heard an awful racket—"

"I'll tell you what happened," Colonel Pettigrew said. "It was Cherokee Hank again, damn his black heart!"

Longarm sighed. Even though he had come here to find Princess Little Feather, he couldn't just ignore the fact that a man had died. If someone had started that stampede, then Alf Culpepper's death could even be regarded as murder. That didn't fall under Longarm's normal jurisdiction, but until the local law showed up, he supposed it wouldn't hurt anything for him to try to sort out some of this mess.

"Colonel," he said to Pettigrew, "suppose you tell me about this fella Cherokee Hank. He's the same as that Henry Trenton you mentioned earlier, ain't he?"

"He's a low-down skunk, that's what he is!" Pettigrew said. "And now he's gone and killed one o' my boys!"

Longarm held up a hand to stop the colonel from going off into a tirade. "Hold on," he said. "We'd best eat this apple one bite at a time. Come on back to your dressing room, Colonel, while your wranglers get those horses back where they're supposed to be." Longarm pointed to Price, Beaumont, and the young woman called Jessamine. "You folks come along, too."

Jessamine looked at him. "Who are you, mister?"

Price answered her. "He's a federal marshal, Jessamine. We'd best do as he says."

"Well, of course," she agreed. To Longarm, she added, "I'll do whatever you want, Marshal."

A woman who looked like she did ought to be careful about making such blanket promises to men, Longarm thought wryly. Some gents would be scoundrels enough to take her up on it. He might have considered it himself under other circumstances, he decided.

Jessamine was mighty pretty with all that blonde hair and peaches-and-cream skin. The thin wrapper she wore clung enticingly to the curves of her body. From the looks of the way her nipples poked against the flimsy fabric, she wasn't wearing much, if anything, underneath it, either. Longarm recalled some of the printing on the flier he had folded up and replaced in his pocket. Jessamine Langley was the name of the show's trick rider. Longarm was sure that was who he was looking at now.

Price kept an arm possessively around Jessamine's shoulders as he gave some orders to the other wranglers. The crowd broke up as most of the men went to drive the horses back to the corrals. With any luck, this time there wouldn't be a stampede. Two of the cowboys stayed behind to keep an eye on the body, not that anyone was likely to disturb it.

The wrangler called Beaumont looked at Longarm and asked in a surly tone, "Why do you want to talk to me?"

"You're a witness," Longarm said curtly.

"No more so than a dozen other fellas."

"Just come on," Longarm snapped. He wasn't in any mood for arguments. This evening had already turned out much differently than he had expected. He had figured he'd get drunk, sleep it off, and go back to Denver on the morning train.

Instead, Katherine Nash had turned up on his doorstep, and her visit had sent him here on a job he considered pretty much a wild-goose chase. Then this business of the stampede and possible murder had popped up. And he still hadn't found out anything about Princess Little Feather! Longarm could feel the night's rest slipping further and further away from him.

Longarm herded the four people back to Colonel Pettigrew's dressing room. Once they were inside, the colonel took another drink from the bottle. This time, he didn't offer to share, and that was a good thing because he drained what was left of the whiskey.

The room was sparsely furnished. The only places to sit were a couple of chairs. Price held one of them for Jessamine, who sat down and folded her hands rather primly in her lap. Longarm nodded for Pettigrew to take the other one. The colonel reversed the chair, straddled it, and rested his arms atop the back of it.

"Tell me about Cherokee Hank," Longarm said again, "and this time leave out the cussing and name-calling and get on with it."

"Sure, I reckon I can do that," Pettigrew said. "But it'll be hard not to express myself about that dingblasted, no-good, cowardly—" He broke off his comments at a hard look from Longarm, then resumed in a more normal voice, "Cherokee Hank is really Henry Trenton, just like you probably guessed, Marshal. But he ain't no more a real Cherokee than you or me. That's just something he calls himself so it'll sound better for the audience."

"He runs another Wild West Show, doesn't he?" Longarm asked. He didn't say anything about Katherine Nash's speculation that the colonel wasn't a real colonel.

Pettigrew's head bobbed up and down. "Yep, that's right. Cherokee Hank's Traveling Circus and Wild West Show. Stole the idea from me, I swear he did. Before that, it was just Trenton's Traveling Circus, and let me tell you, it was a real raggedy-ass outfit."

Again, Longarm could have made some comment about both of them being inspired by Bill Cody's show, but he didn't. Instead, he said, "So you think Trenton's out to cause you trouble because he runs a rival outfit?"

"Of course! Entertainin' the public is pretty much a cut-throat business, Marshal. But there's still rules, and Hank ignores 'em when it suits him, which is all the time."

"So when you started having problems, you just naturally figured Trenton was behind them?"

Pettigrew held up a pudgy hand and counted off the incidents. "A Chinese laundry in New York lost half our costumes while they was bein' cleaned. In Philadelphia somebody stole some of our saddles. In St. Louis we didn't have any place to stay because somebody wired the hotel to cancel our reservations. And that's not even mentionin' all the times our fliers have been torn down, our advance man jumped and beaten up, and our people threatened. I tell you, Marshal, it's plain as the nose on my face! Hank wants to run me out of business so he'll have one less competitor."

Price said quietly, "I never thought he'd have somebody killed, though."

"That stampede might not have been meant to kill anybody," Longarm mused. "If somebody started it on purpose, they may have just intended to cause a headache for you boys. Maybe they hoped some of the horses would be hurt. That would damage the show, wouldn't it?"

"Sure as shootin' it would!" Pettigrew said. "You can't put on a wild west show without a full complement of horses. And I sure can't afford to buy any more mounts right now."

Longarm recalled the comment from Kurt Schilling earlier in the evening about Pettigrew not being much of a businessman. Longarm had seen the evidence of that himself. It was clear that the colonel's operation was on pretty shaky ground. If someone—say, a rival such as Cherokee Hank Trenton—could cause enough trouble for the troupe, it was entirely likely that Pettigrew would be forced to shut down.

"Who's that Schilling fella who was in here earlier?" Longarm asked.

"My paymaster and bookkeeper," Pettigrew replied. "You want me to fetch him?"

Longarm shook his head. Maybe later, he would talk to Schilling and confirm his guess about the show's precarious financial position. Or maybe by that time, the local law would have taken over the investigation, and Longarm would be free to go on about his own business.

There were a couple more things nagging at him. He turned to Ben Price and said, "You sent Culpepper back to the arena from the corrals?"

"That's right." Price's face flushed. "You're not sayin' I intended for him to get hurt, are you, Marshal?" He cast a hard glance toward Beaumont. "I expect that from some people, but not from a lawman."

Longarm didn't answer Price's question. "What was that about a saddle somebody lost?"

Jessamine Langley spoke up. "I'm afraid that was me, Marshal. It's a special saddle I use in my trick riding act."

"*You* didn't lose it," Beaumont said. "It was my job to take it back to the tack room."

Longarm looked at Beaumont. "So you said something to Price about the saddle not being where it was supposed to be?"

"Yeah." Beaumont grimaced. "Damn it, now you sound like you're suspicious of *me*!"

"I'm suspicious of nobody—and everybody," Longarm said. "That's what comes of carrying a badge. I got to admit, though, this ain't really my bailiwick. Somebody had better go for the Kansas City law."

Price said, "I already sent one of my boys, when I was tellin' them to round up those horses and get them back in the corral."

Longarm nodded, glad to hear that. This affair had the makings of a first-class mess, and he wanted no part of it.

Pettigrew frowned and said, "Ben, what was that you were sayin' about some sort o' flash startin' the stampede?"

Price glanced at Beaumont again, and Longarm recalled that Beaumont had denied seeing any such flash. "I saw it," Price said flatly. "Like lightning goin' off, but without any thunder. It was enough to spook those horses and start 'em runnin'."

"What could cause something like that?" Beaumont asked scornfully.

Longarm could think of one thing: a photographer's flash powder. When that phosphorus went off, there was often a whoosh, but no bang.

"I don't know what caused it," Price said stubbornly, "but I know I saw it."

Longarm said, "If you're right, then the stampede was started deliberately. That would sure make Culpepper's death murder."

A new voice spoke from the doorway. "And that makes it my business."

Longarm turned and saw a thick-bodied man of medium height coming in the door. He wore a gray tweed suit and a derby. His face was lined and weathered, and his hair was iron-gray. He looked tough enough to chew nails.

"I'm Lieutenant McClain from the Kansas City police. We received word there'd been a death here." The officer looked at Longarm. "Who're you?"

Longarm tried not to sigh. People kept asking him that question tonight. Once again, he produced his badge and identification.

McClain grunted. "Federal man, eh? Is this related to a case you're working on?"

"Only indirectly," Longarm said. "I just happened to be here when the stampede started. Thought it wouldn't hurt if I asked a few questions."

The detective grunted again. Longarm couldn't tell from his impassive face if he resented the fact that a federal lawman was meddling in a local affair or not. McClain said, "Well, then, you might as well fill me in."

Longarm did so, quickly sketching in the events of the past hour or so with a few added comments from Pettigrew, Price, and Beaumont. Jessamine sat quietly, seemingly not bothered at all by the fact that she was so scantily clad in a room full of men.

When the story was finished, McClain shook his head. "This is Kansas City," he said. "This is a civilized town. People don't get killed anymore by *stampedes*, for God's sake. This isn't the West."

Longarm clamped his mouth shut. He didn't much care for the detective's attitude. Longarm had seen civilization, and he had seen the frontier. Both had things to recommend them, and both had drawbacks. But if he'd been forced to choose, he would have picked the frontier any day. That was why he had left West-by-God Virginia after the War and followed Horace Greeley's advice. It was a decision Longarm had never regretted.

"I suppose I'd better take a look at the body and at the corral where the stampede started," McClain went on. He gave Longarm a curt nod. "Thanks for your help, Marshal."

The message was plain: Longarm was being dismissed and could go on about his business, whatever that was, as long as it was somewhere away from here. Out of sheer cussedness, Longarm was tempted for a moment to declare that he could hang around for a while and give McClain a hand, but he *did* have a job of his own waiting for him. So he returned McClain's nod and said, "Good luck, Lieutenant." He couldn't resist adding, "If you need me, I'll be around until day after tomorrow."

McClain didn't say anything. Longarm nodded his farewell to Colonel Pettigrew and the other three members of the troupe who were in the dressing room, then left.

He paused outside the arena to draw a deep breath and then light a cheroot. Katherine Nash had said that the members of the Wild West Show were staying at The Cattlemen's Hotel, so he supposed that was where he would find Princess Little Feather. He wondered if he would also find someone guarding her room. If that proved to be the case, it would be one more indication that maybe she was really the daughter of that Pawnee chief, Lame Bear, after all.

Earlier, Longarm had been able to catch a hansom cab to bring him out here to the fairgrounds. Now, this late in the evening, that was going to be impossible. The hotel was within walking distance, though, and it was a nice night. Longarm had done enough cowboying so that he didn't like to walk anywhere that he could ride, but he didn't mind being afoot as much as most punchers did. And his high-topped boots had low enough heels so that if he was lucky he wouldn't wear any blisters on his feet by the time he reached the hotel.

Besides, the walk would give him time to think.

From everything Longarm had heard, Pettigrew might well be right about Cherokee Hank Trenton causing the trouble that had plagued the show during its tour. Of course, it was possible that they'd simply had more than their share of bad luck. Longarm had learned over his years as a lawman, though, not to believe too much in coincidence or even in luck. Whatever happened, there was usually a reason somewhere behind it, if a fella just knew where to look. Still, pure chance sometimes *did* play a hand in events, enough so that it couldn't ever be ruled out entirely.

Folks generally had only a limited number of reasons for causing trouble for other folks: love and lust, power and money. Sometimes fear or revenge. Longarm had seen the friction between Ben Price and the wrangler called Beaumont, but he didn't know the reason for it, nor if the trouble between the men could be related in any way to the stampede and the death of Alf Culpepper. The whole thing reminded him of the brands that Mexican ranchers used on their cattle, a mess of lines so tangled up they were known by the term "skillet of snakes."

That was a good way to describe human emotions and the things that often resulted from them, Longarm reflected: a dadblamed skillet of snakes.

He tossed the butt of his cheroot away, looked up, and saw that he had arrived at The Cattlemen's Hotel. The lobby was still brightly lit, and although the dining room was no doubt closed by now, the bar would still be open. Longarm thought that he might stop in there for a drink—*after* he'd talked to Princess Little Feather.

He went inside and identified himself to the slick-haired gent at the desk, then said, "I need to talk to the gal who calls herself Princess Little Feather."

"I believe the princess has retired for the evening," the clerk said, pushing his rimless spectacles higher on his nose.

"That don't make no nevermind to me," said Longarm. "This is United States government business."

"It can't wait until morning?"

As a matter of fact, it probably could, Longarm thought, but he hadn't started out in the best of moods and by now

33

he was feeling positively fractious. He said tersely, "Just tell me the lady's room number."

The clerk swallowed nervously. "Twenty-seven. It's upstairs, in the back."

Longarm nodded. "Much obliged."

He climbed the stairs without looking back, and it took him only a few minutes to locate room twenty-seven. Pausing for a moment in front of the door, he listened intently for any sound that might be coming from the room. He didn't hear anything. Nor was there a guard posted in the hallway, as there would have been if the princess was really a prisoner. Longarm lifted his hand and rapped sharply on the door.

Several seconds passed without a response, and Longarm was about to knock again when a woman's sleepy voice called from inside, "Who is it?"

Well, he'd woken her up, Longarm thought. And she just sounded sleepy, not like she was in any sort of danger or desperate to get away. A wild-goose chase, just like he'd thought.

"Federal marshal, ma'am," he said, leaning closer to the door so that his voice would carry through it. "If you're Princess Little Feather, I need to talk to you for a minute."

"Hold on."

Longarm waited. A moment later he heard the soft pad of feet across the floor, and a key rattled in the lock. The knob turned and the door swung back. The woman who opened it looked out at Longarm and said, "I'm Princess Little Feather. What can I do for you?"

Longarm's eyes widened in surprise. He knew one thing just by looking at her.

Princess Little Feather sure as hell wasn't a Pawnee.

Chapter 4

She wasn't even an Indian, not unless there was some tribe Longarm had never heard of that was native to the Ould Sod. With that mass of red curls tumbling around her shoulders and the green eyes peering at him out of a lightly freckled face, "Princess Little Feather" was undoubtedly Irish.

Longarm wondered for a second if he had come to the wrong room, then he recalled that this woman had not only answered to the Indian name, she had even introduced herself that way. What in blazes was going on here?

The redhead smiled a little at her visitor's puzzlement. "I don't blame you for being confused," she said. "I don't look much like a savage, do I?"

"Maybe a Hibernian one," Longarm answered with a smile of his own. It was hard not to smile at a gal as pretty as this one.

For the third time this evening, Longarm found himself looking at a true beauty. This woman was in her early twenties, he judged, about the same age as Jessamine Langley and a little younger than Katherine Nash. She wore a dark green robe that went well with her eyes and hair color. Her hair was disarrayed from sleep, but Longarm had always liked the way that looked on a woman. The robe was bulkier than the thin wrapper Jessamine had been wearing at the arena, so Longarm couldn't tell how well this woman was shaped, but he was willing to bet her body would be mighty easy on the eyes, just like the rest of her.

She held her hand out and said, "Perhaps I should properly introduce myself. My name is Maureen Mullaney."

Longarm could believe that; the name certainly suited her. He took her hand briefly, noting the surprising strength in the long, slender fingers. "Custis Long. Like I said, I'm a U.S. deputy marshal."

"And you want to speak to me about what, Marshal?"

Suddenly the whole thing seemed so damned silly to Longarm that he hated to admit to her why he was here. But she was curious, naturally enough, and he supposed that since he had come this far, he might as well finish the job.

"You don't look much like a Pawnee princess," he said.

"That's because I'm not. It's just a role I play." Maureen Mullaney's smile widened. "You'd be amazed what a transformation a black wig, a little makeup, and a buckskin outfit can accomplish."

"Why the Indian getup?"

Maureen shrugged. "It was Colonel Pettigrew's idea. He's such an old fraud that he doesn't think anyone else should be who they really are, either." She shook her head. "I still don't see what this has to do with the federal government, though. Is there some law against pretending to be a Pawnee princess?"

"Not that I know of," Longarm admitted. "But you see, one of their chiefs, a gent called Lame Bear, lost his daughter a while back, and after he saw one of the posters advertising the Colonel's Wild West Show, he got it in his head that you were her. Since I was here in Kansas City already, the Bureau of Indian Affairs asked me to check into it for them."

"Oh. Well, I'm sorry about Chief Lame Bear's daughter." She sounded genuinely sympathetic. "But as you can see . . ." She spread her hands and indicated herself. "I'm not even an Indian."

"No, ma'am, you're not." Longarm reached up and tugged on the brim of his hat as he nodded to her. "Good night to you."

As he started to turn away, Maureen lifted a hand. "Marshal . . . ?"

Longarm paused. "Yes, ma'am?"

"Why don't you come inside? Now that I'm awake, I know it's going to be a while before I'm sleepy again."

"I wouldn't want to intrude."

Maureen shook her head. "You wouldn't be intruding at all. In fact, I could use the company. And you *are* the one who woke me up," she added.

"Well . . . I wouldn't be much of a gentleman if I turned down a lady's invitation, would I?"

"Are you a gentleman, Marshal Long?"

"I try to be," Longarm said.

"A gentleman always obliges a lady."

"Yes, ma'am," Longarm said.

He was the luckiest son of a bitch on the whole damned planet, Longarm thought as he pumped his hips back and forth and drove his manhood deeper into the hot, wet opening between Maureen Mullaney's widespread thighs.

Most fellas would go their entire lives without being invited into the bed of a beautiful woman less than an hour after meeting her. Longarm wasn't sure what it was that led him to stumble into situations such as this on a fairly regular basis. Not that he was complaining. After the evening he'd had—hell, after the last couple of days—bedding Maureen was just what he needed to take the edge off.

"Oh, God, yes!" Maureen panted as she tossed her head back and forth on the pillow. "Give me all of it, Custis! I want all of that magnificent thing inside me!"

Longarm lifted himself higher and drove deeper. He balanced on his knees and grasped Maureen's legs, raising them until he could rest them on his shoulders. Then he

37

grabbed her hips to steady her as he began plunging into her in a rhythm that grew increasingly faster. She turned her head and bit down on the corner of the pillow to keep from screaming out her pleasure.

It had started out simply enough. The two of them had gone into Maureen's hotel room and sat down, Maureen on the edge of the bed and Longarm in an armchair, and Longarm had told her more about Chief Lame Bear and the daughter who had disappeared during a battle with the cavalry. Maureen had been sympathetic, for both the chief and the little girl, whose fate was still unknown.

Longarm had considered telling her about the stampede at the arena, in vague hopes of finding out more about the troubles plaguing Colonel Pettigrew's troupe, but before he could get around to that, Maureen had offered him a glass of brandy. "I'm afraid it's all I have on hand," she'd said.

Brandy was fine with Longarm. They'd each had a glass, and Maureen had sat back on the bed, crossing her legs so that the robe fell away from her calves. And nice calves they were, too, Longarm had noted.

"I'm one of these people who have a terrible time getting back to sleep once I've been woken up," she said again.

"I'm sorry I had to disturb you," Longarm had said.

Maureen waved a hand. "Please, don't worry about it. I'm enjoying talking to you, Marshal."

"Call me Custis," he'd suggested.

Maureen smiled. "Custis. An unusual name, but it fits you. Do you go by anything else?"

He'd shrugged. "Some folks call me Longarm."

"I'll bet *that* fits you, too."

Damned if she wasn't flirting with him, he thought. And he was enjoying it. The brandy had perked him up a mite. The way that robe kept falling farther and farther open was enough to make him forget how tired he'd been, as well. The top of the garment was gaping some now, enough to reveal the beginning of an enticing valley between two swells of bare, creamy flesh.

"You know, Custis," Maureen had said, "there is one thing that almost always helps me sleep."

"Well, ma'am, if there's anything I can do—"

"To start with, you can come over here and kiss me."

Longarm downed the little bit of brandy that was left in the bottom of the glass, then stood up and set the empty on a small side table. Maureen watched him with green eyes that had taken on a smoky tinge. Her lips were curved in a faint smile as he came toward her.

He'd taken off his hat and sat down on the bed beside her, and the mattress sagged just enough so that their hips came together. Even through their clothes, Longarm could feel the heat coming off Maureen's body. He'd leaned closer, slipping an arm around her waist. She tilted her head back, eyes heavy-lidded now, lips slightly parted in anticipation. Longarm's mouth came down on hers.

Right from the start, she'd been one hell of a kisser. Her mouth opened wider in hungry urgency, and her tongue darted hotly into Longarm's mouth. He met it with his own tongue, and they began thrusting and circling in a duel that had no losers, only winners. His arm tightened around her waist, and he pulled her closer. His other hand came up and slipped inside the robe, cupping and squeezing her right breast. He thumbed the hard nipple, the caress drawing a tiny shudder from Maureen.

Finally, she pulled her head back and said breathlessly, "That . . . that's a good start. But I'm not feeling sleepy yet."

Longarm's hand dropped to the robe's belt that was tied around Maureen's waist. One quick tug had it untied, and then he slowly spread the robe open so that her breasts were revealed.

They rode full and high on her chest, firm with youth. Faint traceries of blue veins were barely visible underneath the smooth, creamy skin. Longarm's eyes had been drawn irresistibly to the large, thick nipples which stood erect and crowned each globe. The ring of brown, slightly puckered flesh that surrounded each nipple was somewhat wider than usual. Longarm hadn't been able to resist the temptation for very long. His head dipped and he popped first one then the other nipple into his mouth, sucking gently at first, then harder as Maureen began to stroke his head.

"Oh!" she'd said with quiet urgency. "Oh, you do that so well, Custis."

He'd stopped sucking and started laving the nipples with his tongue instead, then took turns drawing as much of each breast into his mouth as he could. While he was doing that, he'd opened the robe the rest of the way, baring her below the waist as well. His face was buried in the valley between the globes of warm flesh and he didn't want to leave them just yet, so he reached down and worked by feel, sliding one hand along the heated softness of an inner thigh until he felt a thick mat of fine-spun hair tickling the back of his hand. Maureen had spread her legs, giving him easy access to her femaleness. He'd cupped the mound at the juncture of her thighs, pressing down on it for a moment, then reached lower and trailed his fingers along the moist lips, finding the little nubbin at the top of the slit and toying with it. Maureen gave a soft cry and fell backward on the bed, spreading her legs even more.

Longarm had slipped to his knees beside the bed. He was still fully dressed except for his hat, and Maureen was nude except for the open robe that was spread out underneath her. There was something erotic about that contrast. Even more arousing was the contrast between the pale, spread-eagled thighs and the thick triangle of dark red hair between them. Longarm hadn't tried to resist the impulses that ran through him. He leaned forward, using his fingers to spread the folds of flesh, then plunged his tongue between them.

Maureen's hips had bounced up off the bed, driving her sex against Longram's face. He managed to keep his tongue inside her and began sliding it up and down. He reached underneath her and grasped the cheeks of her bottom, holding firmly to them and pulling her even closer. With one finger he explored the valley between the cheeks, prodding

40

at the tight brown ring until it opened enough to let him slide his finger inside. Maureen moaned in passion at the intimate caress. By that time, Longarm had been pretty much lost in a sea of lust and need, but a small part of his brain was still working enough to hope that she wouldn't get too loud and cause the other guests to complain downstairs.

Longarm had stayed busy with fingers and tongue for several minutes, bringing Maureen to a higher and higher pitch until she'd clamped her thighs around his head and damn near strangled him with the frenzied strength of the climax that gripped her. When her legs finally fell open again, he was able to lift his head and look up at her. From this angle, he had a good view of her large breasts rising and falling rapidly as she tried to catch her breath. "That was so good," she said in a half whisper. "I think I can go to sleep now."

That had brought Longarm quickly upright so that he could see her face. He was so hard he was aching, and it was intolerable to think that Maureen might just roll over and go to sleep now, of all times. As soon as he saw the wicked grin on her face, he knew that she hadn't been serious with her comment.

"You were just funning me," he accused.

"Yes, but I had you worried for a minute, didn't I?" Still breathing hard, she'd sat up and reached for the buttons of his trousers. "You don't think I'd go to sleep without getting a good look at what you've got in there, do you? From the size of that bulge, I'd say it's quite impressive."

Longarm slipped off his coat, vest, tie, and shirt while Maureen was unfastening his trousers. He took his gun belt off, too, and half-turned to place the cross-draw rig on a chair. When he turned back, Maureen pushed his trousers down. Longarm was wearing only the bottom half of a pair of long underwear, so Maureen had hooked her fingers in the waistband and pulled them down over his thighs as well.

The freedom his shaft experienced when it finally was

released from its confinement was intoxicating. From her position sitting on the edge of the bed, Maureen was able to get a good look at it, all right. She murmured, "Oh, my. Can a normal woman get all of that inside her?" She gave a little laugh and answered her own question. "I suppose we'll find out in a little while."

She used both hands to grasp the shaft and leaned over to take the head inside her mouth. Her lips stretched wide around it. Her tongue explored the opening at the tip. Longarm had closed his eyes and exerted all his willpower to keep from spurting his seed into her mouth.

As Maureen began a steady sucking, she reached down with one hand to cup the heavy sacs that hung underneath the thick pole of male flesh. She rolled them back and forth in her palm, then squeezed them, none too gently. Longarm's hips had automatically thrust forward, so that Maureen's mouth was filled even more than before.

He knew he had brought her to climax with his mouth, but he didn't want her to return the favor. Not just yet, anyway. He wanted the first time to be with him buried deep in her belly. He combed his fingers through her thick red hair, then slid his hands around to cup her cheeks as she sucked him. He pulled up, so that she had to tilt her head back and look at him.

"Better hold off," he warned her, "else you'll get a mouthful. And I reckon both of us would rather finish off the other way."

She'd nodded and given his shaft a last lick as she took her mouth away. Again she lay back on the bed and spread her legs. "Now, Custis," she urged. "Do it to me now."

He hadn't wasted any time getting rid of the rest of his clothes and giving her what she wanted. As aroused as he was, he'd figured that he wouldn't last very long, but to his surprise, he found that he was able to postpone his own culmination. Maureen had come a couple of times since he'd penetrated her, and now she was building up for yet another shattering climax. Longarm felt his seed boiling up

42

and knew he wouldn't be able to hold off this time. The moment had arrived.

As Maureen began shaking and writhing and clutching at him, he drove into her as deeply as he possibly could and let go, flooding her inside with spurt after scalding spurt. He trembled with the force of the explosions as he emptied himself in her.

Finally, it was over, and both of them came gliding down from the crest of the peak they had just scaled. Maureen lay panting, eyes closed, while Longarm lightly kissed her lips and nose and jaw and throat.

Damn, he loved women! he thought, and never more than at a moment such as this. He loved the way they felt in his arms, the smell of their hair, the warmth of their breath, the softness of their embrace. Some things just flatout never grew old, and this was one of them.

He was mighty lucky that his original plans for the evening had gotten themselves changed, he told himself.

But as he rolled to the side so that he was sprawled on the bed beside Maureen Mullaney, the earlier events came back to him, jarringly elbowing their way into his brain once more.

Maureen curled onto her side and moved against him so that she could rest her head on his shoulder. Longarm put his arm around her, luxuriating in the feel of her smooth skin as he ran his palm along her flank to the swell of her hip. He would have enjoyed the sensation even more if he hadn't had nagging questions percolating around in the back of his mind.

"That was wonderful," Maureen whispered. Now she sounded genuinely drowsy. Given half a chance, she would probably doze off.

Hating himself for it, Longarm said, "I went out to the arena earlier tonight and talked to Colonel Pettigrew."

"I thought you must have," Maureen murmured. "How else would you have known I was here?"

Longarm didn't answer that question, figuring Maureen

wasn't really expecting an answer. Instead, he said, "Something happened while I was out there."

Something in his tone of voice must have penetrated Maureen's passion-sated mood. She lifted her head and turned it so that she could look at him. "Some sort of trouble?"

"There was a stampede after the show," Longarm told her. "The horses got spooked and bolted back down the aisle between the corrals and the arena."

Maureen came up on an elbow. She frowned worriedly and asked, "Was anyone hurt?"

"One of the wranglers, a fella named Alf Culpepper. He was trampled. Never had a chance."

Maureen's other hand went to her mouth in horror. "Oh, my God! Alf . . . Alf's dead?"

Longarm nodded grimly. "I'm sorry, Maureen. I know this sure ain't the right time or place to be breaking news like this—"

She sat up sharply. "I can't believe it. I just can't believe it."

Longarm sat up beside her. "This fella Alf, was he a friend of yours?"

"I didn't know him all that well, I suppose. I don't do any riding in my act, so I'm not around the wranglers very much. But of course I *did* know him and like him." Maureen shook her head. "This is terrible, just terrible." Realization hit her, and she turned to look again at Longarm. "The stampede wasn't an accident, was it?"

"What makes you say that?"

"Because this is just the sort of thing that Cherokee Hank would do," Maureen said. "He's been causing trouble for us ever since we left on this tour. You *do* know about Cherokee Hank?"

"And his Traveling Circus and Wild West Show," Longarm said. "Yeah, Colonel Pettigrew had a few things to say about ol' Cherokee Hank."

"Somebody has to stop him. I was afraid that it was just a matter of time until someone got killed." Something else occurred to Maureen. "You're a lawman. Surely you can do something about this."

"A policeman named McClain, from the Kansas City police force, is investigating."

"I don't trust these local lawmen," Maureen said without hesitation. "But you could stop Trenton and see to it that he pays for what he's done."

"I'm out of my bailiwick," Longarm began.

"If you don't do it, Custis, no one will. But I trust you to see that justice is done."

"You just met me a little while ago," Longarm pointed out.

"I'm a good judge of character." Maureen glanced down at her nudity. "Otherwise, we wouldn't have been doing what we've been doing. I know you're an honest man, and I know you won't let murder go unpunished."

Damn it, he wished she hadn't put it like that. Appealing to his sense of justice was sure enough one way to get him to poke his nose into something, whether it really belonged there or not.

"I suppose I could ask around a mite more," he said slowly, "though I reckon it's likely Lieutenant McClain won't much cotton to having another lawman traipsing around in his territory."

Maureen put her arms around him and said, "I knew you'd understand, Custis." She kissed him, hard and urgent. "I knew you were a good man as soon as I saw you . . . and good at what you do, too . . ."

She reached down to massage his shaft, and to her surprise as well as Longarm's own, she found it swelling again in her hand.

"Oh, yes," Maureen breathed. "Very good at the things you do . . ."

Chapter 5

What with one thing and another—most of them having to do with the fascinating skills displayed by Maureen Mullaney—Longarm didn't get back to the hotel where he was staying until just about dawn the next morning. This place wasn't as fancy as The Cattlemen's Hotel, of course, since Uncle Sam was paying for it. The clerk behind the counter didn't pay much attention as Longarm came in and asked for his key. He didn't care one way or the other what time the big lawman was getting back in.

Longarm knew there was a Western Union office right down the street; he'd wired Billy Vail from it the previous afternoon after delivering Rollie Ashdown to the army guard detail. He went upstairs to his room, intending to freshen up and then send another telegram to Denver.

When he reached his door, however, he stopped short. A frown creased his forehead as he studied the tiny gap between the door and the jamb. Before leaving to go downstairs and meet Katherine Nash in the dining room the night before, he had followed his usual cautious habit and placed a matchstick in the door, close to the floor so it wouldn't be easily noticed. The match was gone now, meaning that someone had opened the door in his absence.

Longarm's hand went to the butt of his Colt. He slipped the revolver from its holster. There might be a perfectly innocent reason someone had gone into his room, but it had been Longarm's experience that perfectly innocent reasons for *anything* in this world were rare. The door key was in his left hand, since another old habit of his was keeping his right hand empty and ready to reach for a gun. He slipped the key into the lock and turned it as quietly as possible.

Then he twisted the knob, threw the door open, and went through it in a rush, crouching low and darting to the side as soon as he was in the room.

His eyes flicked left, right, left again. No one in sight, and there was nowhere in the room a bushwhacker could hide unless it was under the bed. Longarm grabbed the mattress and threw it aside so that he could peer down through the bed slats. The Colt in his hand menaced nothing except a couple of dust balls, however.

Longarm grunted. A part of him wanted to feel foolish for reacting as he had, but at the same time, *someone* had been in this room, and he'd had no choice except to proceed as if the intruder were waiting in there to ventilate him.

He holstered the gun and put the mattress back on the bed. Then he shut the door, thankful that none of the other hotel guests had wandered by in the hallway while he was pointing his gun at dust balls.

He looked around. He hadn't brought his saddle and Winchester on this trip, since he'd planned to spend most of his time on a train, but he had his war bag with him. It was propped in a corner. He picked it up, opened the drawstring at the top, and poked through the contents: a couple of clean shirts, some underwear, and a nearly full box of .44 cartridges. None of it had been disturbed, and Longarm wasn't sure why anyone would have wanted to search the bag in the first place.

A sneak thief, maybe. That was a possibility. A would-be robber could have gotten in here, poked around a little, realized there was nothing worth stealing, and left. Longarm thought about it and decided that was the explanation that made the most sense.

But if that was the case, why did something in his gut tell him it wasn't right?

Lacking any other option at the moment, he went back to his original plan. He washed his face and shaved using the basin of water on the chest of drawers, then put on a fresh shirt and left the hotel again, without saying anything to the clerk downstairs about someone getting into his room. For all Longarm knew, the clerk himself could be the guilty party. He had access to a key, after all.

Despite the early hour, the Western Union office was already open, the operator sitting at his key pounding out messages in a competent hand. Longarm came up to the counter and nodded at the man. He picked up a message blank and a stub of pencil and began printing.

A few minutes later, the operator sent the message for Longarm.

TO CHIEF MARSHAL VAIL DENVER STOP REMAINING IN
KC AT REQUEST OF BIA AGENT NASH STOP NEED INFO ON
COLONEL JASPER PETTIGREW AND HENRY TRENTON STOP
RETURN TO DENVER INDEFINITE STOP LONG.

Billy would probably wonder what his deputy had stumbled into, but it was too complicated to go into in a telegram, Longarm knew. Besides, investigating the trouble between Pettigrew and Trenton wasn't really his responsibility, and when Longarm finally got back to Denver, Vail would probably have some choice comments about that. But for the time being, what Billy didn't know wouldn't hurt either of them.

"You want to wait for the reply, Marshal?" the operator asked.

Longarm shook his head. "It may take a while. I'll come by later and see if you've heard back from Denver."

He left the office and strode toward The Cattlemen's Hotel, which was several blocks away. The sun was up by now, already giving promise of a warm spring day.

Longarm figured Colonel Pettigrew and most of the other members of the Wild West Show would still be asleep, but as he entered the lobby and passed by the entrance to the dining room, he heard a familiar gravelly voice call, "Marshal Long!" Longarm turned to see Pettigrew sitting at one of the tables in the dining room, along with the bald-headed bookkeeper, Kurt Schilling. The colonel motioned for Longarm to join them.

He did so, walking across the dining room to the table and pulling out a chair. "Morning," he said with a nod to Pettigrew and Schilling. "Didn't expect you folks to be up and about yet."

"You are," Pettigrew pointed out. "Me, I always like to get a good early start on the day. When you get to be my age, you realize there ain't that many hours left to you."

"Nonsense," Schilling said. "You will outlive us all, Jasper." He seemed to be in a friendlier mood today. He turned to Longarm and went on, "How are you, Marshal?"

"Fine, I reckon. Was there any more trouble out at the arena last night after I left?"

"Nope, thank the Lord," Pettigrew said. "Say, you better get a surroundin' of this chuck. It's mighty good." He used the fork in his hand to point to the pile of sausage, hash browns, fried eggs, and flapjacks piled high on the plate in front of him. In contrast, Schilling had only a cup of coffee in front of him.

Longarm realized it had been a long time since he'd eaten the night before, and his amorous activities with Maureen Mullaney had used up a lot of energy. He caught the eye of a waitress in a blue-checked gingham dress and white apron and said to her, "I'll have what the colonel's having, and bring a fresh pot of Arbuckle's."

Pettigrew chuckled. "Sure you can keep up with me, son? I've got a hollow leg."

"I'll give it a try," Longarm said with a smile. He looked at Schilling again. "So this is payday, eh?"

"You remember the conversation with Asa Wilburn last night, I see," Schilling commented. "*Ja*, today the performers will receive their wages. Luckily the audience was large enough last night to enable us to pay them."

Colonel Pettigrew frowned. "Dang it, Kurt, you make it sound like we're livin' from show to show and barely makin' ends meet."

"This is true, *nicht wahr?*"

"I told you, don't talk that Dutchy talk at me," Pettigrew snapped. "I know good and well you can talk American just fine."

Schilling shrugged. "My apologies. The hour is early yet, and I did not sleep well. It is easy to fall into old habits."

"I hate to bring this up over breakfast," Longarm said, "but did Lieutenant McClain find out anything more about the stampede that killed Culpepper?"

Pettigrew shook his head. "Hell, no. That fella couldn't find his own ass with both hands. Didn't stop him from keepin' us there at the arena for hours whilst he asked questions and went pokin' around the place."

Longarm had no real evidence to go by, but he suspected that the local lawman wasn't as ineffective as Pettigrew made him out to be. Still, that was something that only time would tell. The waitress arrived with Longarm's food and the pot of coffee, and he waited until he'd put himself on the outside of some of it before resuming the conversation.

"I spoke to Princess Little Feather last night and cleared up that matter," Longarm said.

Pettigrew grinned. "Bet you was surprised when you saw she ain't really an Indian."

"You could have told me that," Longarm pointed out dryly.

"Shoot, you're a smart young feller. I knew you could figure it out once you saw all that red hair." Pettigrew drank some coffee. "Goin' to tell me what that was all about?"

"A case of mistaken identity," Longarm said simply. "Somebody thought Miss Mullaney was really somebody else, and I was checking on that." If the colonel wanted more of the details, Maureen could tell him.

Pettigrew seemed satisfied by Longarm's answer, however. He said, "She's quite a looker, ain't she?"

"Gorgeous," Schilling murmured. For a moment, he had a faraway look in his eyes, and Longarm wondered if he was thinking about Maureen. She was lovely enough to get under the skin of any man, even a cold-blooded Prussian bookkeeper.

"She's a nice gal," Longarm said. "I told her about what happened last night. She was pretty upset."

"I reckon so. Maureen's got a soft spot in her heart for just about ever'body with the show."

Schilling's mouth tightened as he listened to the colonel's statement. Longarm noticed that and found himself wondering again. He wondered if Schilling had made advances to Maureen in the past and been rejected.

"She seems to think that Henry Trenton is behind what happened, too."

Pettigrew's fist thumped on the table, making some of the other diners look around. "Dadgum right he is! He's to blame for what happened to poor Alf."

"You think Ben Price was right about seeing some sort of flash that set off the stampede?"

"Well . . . that detective fella didn't find no evidence of it, but yeah, I think Ben was right."

"Perhaps the stampede was started in some other fashion," Schilling put in. "Could one of the wranglers have done something to . . . how do you say it . . . spook the horses?"

Pettigrew looked at the bookkeeper with a frown. "Now why in tarnation would anybody do that? All those boys were Alf's pards."

"Perhaps Mr. Culpepper was not really the intended target."

Schilling's quiet words made Longarm frown, too, as he turned them over in his head. Schilling could be on to something. Longarm thought back over everything he had heard the night before.

"There's bad blood between Price and that hombre Beaumont," he said after a moment. "A fella'd have to be blind not to see that."

"And Tom Beaumont told Price about Miss Langley's missing saddle," Schilling said.

Longarm looked at him. "How do you know that?"

Schilling leaned toward Pettigrew. "The Colonel told me all about the unfortunate incident, of course."

Pettigrew leaned forward in his chair. "Hold on just a dadblamed minute," he rumbled. "Are you sayin', Kurt, that Beaumont told Ben Price about the saddle, hopin' that Ben would go lookin' for it and get caught in the stampede?"

Schilling's shoulders rose and fell in a shrug. "Not at all. I was simply advancing the idea as a plausible theory."

"Makes sense, all right," Longarm said as he scraped his thumbnail along the line of his jaw. "I ain't sure how likely it is, though. It'd take some planning to do something like that, not to mention quite a bit of luck. But still, as a theory, I reckon we can't say it didn't happen that way."

"No, sir," Pettigrew insisted. "If that stampede was deliberate, it was Cherokee Hank who done it. I'm sure of it."

Longarm was beginning to get the idea that if it rained later today, Pettigrew would blame Cherokee Hank Trenton for every drop. He asked, "Why do Price and Beaumont have burrs under their saddles for each other?"

"A woman, what else?" Schilling said with a faint smile.

The light dawned on Longarm. "Miss Jessamine," he said.

Pettigrew glowered across the table. "Tom Beaumont used to be sweet on Jessamine, that's true enough, I reckon. But that's been over and done with for quite a while. Jessamine's sweet on Ben now."

"Didn't look to me like Beaumont had gotten over it very well, either."

Pettigrew shook his head. "I just ain't gonna believe it. The folks in my show don't go around tryin' to kill each other."

Whether the colonel wanted to believe it or not, Longarm figured the theory advanced by Kurt Schilling was indeed possible. Beaumont might have been responsible for the stampede, intending for Ben Price to be the one who was trampled. Alf Culpepper's death, therefore, could have been both an accident—and murder.

Longarm polished off the last of his flapjacks and washed them down with another cup of the hot, black, strong coffee. As he placed the cup on its saucer, he said, "I think I might just look into this business after all."

"You're goin' to investigate the trouble we've been havin'?" Pettigrew asked eagerly.

Longarm shrugged. "I'll see what I can root out."

"You'd better start by goin' to see that scoundrel Cherokee Hank. That's where you'll find the one who's to blame for everything."

"Is Trenton's show in town?" Longarm asked, slightly surprised. He wouldn't have thought there would be room for more than one Wild West Show at a time in a place like Kansas City.

"Damn right. He's always doggin' our trail. They got into town yesterday, and the first show's tonight."

"But you're still performing at the arena," Longarm said.

"Trenton's got his own tent. His show used to be just a plain circus, you know. All he needs is a big empty field on the edge of town, and he's in business."

"Maybe I'll pay him a visit tonight."

"You do and you'll find the killer, mark my words."

It seemed more likely to Longarm that if Trenton actually was responsible for the problems plaguing Pettigrew's show, he was paying off somebody who was already working for the colonel. Sabotage was always easier when it was carried out by somebody on the inside. Pettigrew was protective about his people, though; his reaction to Kurt Schilling's theory about Beaumont proved that. He wouldn't want to believe that any member of his troupe would betray him.

So if that turned out to be the case, Longarm thought, he would need solid proof before Pettigrew would believe him. The same was true for the local authorities.

Billy Vail wasn't going to be happy when he found out Longarm had been hanging around Kansas City playing detective. But hell, sometimes a case just got under a man's skin, Longarm told himself. Sometimes the questions were too intriguing, the need to find the answers too compelling to ignore.

And the fact that he would undoubtedly see Maureen Mullaney again probably had something to do with his decision, too, he admitted. He resolved then and there to continue taking advantage of the big meals in The Cattlemen's dining room whenever possible.

With Maureen around, Longarm was going to need to keep up his strength.

Chapter 6

Kurt Schilling finished his coffee and left the dining room before Longarm and Colonel Pettigrew, explaining that he needed to prepare the payroll for the members of the troupe. Longarm lingered over his Arbuckle's, and so did the colonel. Pettigrew continued grousing about Cherokee Hank. Longarm tried to ease his mind by saying, "I'll be heading out there in a little while to have a talk with Trenton."

"Good. Just don't believe anything that rapscallion tells you."

Longarm indulged some idle curiosity and asked, "Where'd you come up with Schilling?"

"He hired on before the tour started," Pettigrew said. "Claims he was some sort o' professor of mathematics at the University of Heidelberg."

Longarm frowned. "I thought from the way he acts that he'd been with the show for a while."

The colonel shook his head and said, "Nope, it's just that Kurt's a friendly feller once you get to know him. I know he don't seem like that at first, but I reckon that's because he's a Prussian and they're sort of naturally stiff-necked. He's dadgum good with numbers, I know that. The gent who used to keep the books and handle the payroll for me retired a few months ago, said he was gettin' too old to go traipsin' around all over the country."

"You ever feel like that?"

Pettigrew looked offended. "Hell, no! I been on the road my whole life, seems like. And when I go, I want 'em to stuff me and prop me up on one o' the wagons, so I can keep travelin'!" He let out a booming laugh.

Longarm chuckled. He said, "I reckon you'd be what they call a stellar attraction, Colonel." Growing more serious, he went on, "I wonder what a professor's doing working as a bookkeeper in a Wild West Show."

"Well, Kurt don't talk much about himself, but I got the idea from hints he dropped that he had some sort o' bust-up with a gal over there where he comes from. I figure he wanted to get as far away from her as possible, so he came to America to make a fresh start."

Longarm nodded. That could be the case, all right, he thought. He'd known plenty of men who took off for the tall and uncut after they'd had their hearts broken by some woman.

He was about to say as much when a sudden gunshot from upstairs made his head jerk up in surprise. For a heart-beat, Longarm thought surely he must be mistaken, that guns didn't go off in fancy hotels like The Cattlemen's in Kansas City. But a second after that, another blast rang out, from the sound of it a different weapon this time.

"What in blue blazes!" Pettigrew exclaimed.

Longarm was already uncoiling from his chair like a giant cat. He broke into a run toward the dining room entrance. By the time he reached it, a third shot had sounded.

Longarm dashed through the lobby toward the stairs, bounding past guests who stood in shocked immobility. He took the stairs three at a time, his long legs carrying him up to the second floor quickly and easily. He didn't know what was going on, and whatever the trouble was, it might not have anything to do with Colonel Pettigrew's Wild West Show. But the thought that Maureen was probably somewhere up here and maybe in danger went through his head anyway.

His Colt was in his hand when he reached the landing.

His free hand caught the stair railing and swung him around in a tight turn. Another shot slammed closer this time. Longarm caught a whiff of burned gunpowder in the air.

As he looked down the corridor, a man came hurrying around a corner. Longarm spotted a gun in the stranger's hand. The man paused and whipped around to snap another shot behind him, down the cross hall. Then he whirled toward Longarm.

"Hold it!" Longarm called as he leveled his Colt.

The stranger wasn't in any mood to be stopped. He threw himself forward, sprawling prone on the floor of the corridor as he fired twice at Longarm. Still on the landing at the top of the stairs, Longarm darted aside as the bullets whined past him. His shoulder smashed into a door, and it was flung open by the impact. Longarm toppled through it, unable to keep his balance.

He heard a woman's scream and knew he had inadvertently busted into somebody's room. A glance toward the bed showed him a man and a woman lying there with the covers pulled up to their necks. Surprise and fear were etched on their faces.

"Stay there!" Longarm snapped to them as he came up into a crouch. He heard more screams and shouts from outside as he dove through the door onto the landing.

He was in time to see the gunman vault over the railing and drop to the lobby below. That was a dangerous move which could easily lead to a broken limb, but the gunman had known that he couldn't take the stairs with Longarm blocking the way. Longarm leaped to the railing and peered down to see the gunman scrambling to his feet, apparently unhurt. No one tried to stop him as he dashed toward the front door of the hotel.

"Hey!" Longarm yelled. He didn't want to shoot anybody in the back, even this fleeing gunman.

He didn't have to. The man twisted around again and flung a shot toward Longarm. The slug missed and smacked into the ceiling above and behind Longarm. Longarm lined the sights of his Colt and squeezed off a shot.

His bullet took the man in the left shoulder, bored down through his torso at an angle, and exploded out of his body just above the right hip. The impact knocked the man into a twisting, spinning fall. The gun slipped from his fingers and went skittering away across the floor of the hotel lobby. The man made no move to retrieve it. In fact, he wasn't moving at all.

A grim look on his face, Longarm clattered down the stairs to the lobby. He kept his pistol trained on the fallen gunman the whole time as he approached the man. Just as Longarm reached the man's side, a rattling breath sounded with finality in his throat. Longarm's mouth quirked in a grimace. So much for being able to question the gunman. The fella was dead.

Longarm went to a knee and checked for a pulse anyway. Finding none, he stood up and holstered his Colt.

"Marshal?"

As keyed up as he was from the exchange of gunfire, Longarm had to make an effort not to spin around and reach for his revolver again. As it was, he was able to turn more slowly. He saw Kurt Schilling standing there at the bottom of the stairs. A small pistol was in the bookkeeper's right hand.

Longarm glanced at the gun that the stranger had dropped. It was a Remington. Longarm had heard both sharp cracks and heavier booms coming from upstairs when the trouble broke out, so it took him only a fleeting second to make the connections. "That was you I heard shooting it out with this hombre, wasn't it?" he said to Schilling.

Schilling opened and closed his mouth a couple of times. He was staring at the body of the gunman lying in a growing pool of blood. Finally, he was able to say, "Is . . . is he dead?"

"Yep," Longarm said. "Now, how about answering my question."

Schilling lifted his right hand and looked at the gun clutched in it as if he had never seen such a thing before. He swallowed hard and said, "I . . . I had no choice."

"You didn't kill him," Longarm said heavily. "I did. And I reckon I'd like to know why."

Schilling took a deep breath. That helped his composure a little. He said, "This man tried to rob me. He was waiting for me when I got back to my room to prepare the payroll."

"He already had his gun out?"

Schilling nodded. "Yes. He threatened me with it."

"But you were packing iron, too?"

The bookkeeper looked at the little pistol again. "I carry a weapon, yes, but I never . . . I never had to use it until today."

"Even though this fella had the drop on you, you pulled your gun anyway and started trading shots with him?"

"I . . . I did not think. I just knew that I could not allow him to steal the payroll money."

Schilling was one of the luckiest sons of bitches on the face of the earth, Longarm thought. By all rights, the gunman should've blown his head off. Longarm tried to remember if the first shot he'd heard had come from the Remington or the little pocket pistol. He decided that Schilling had gotten the first shot off.

"So when you put up a fight, he tried to run?"

Schilling nodded again. "That is correct. He shot at me, I shot at him. Evidently, neither of us hit our targets."

Schilling was pretty much himself again, though he still seemed a little shaky. Longarm pointed at the pistol in the bookkeeper's hand and said, "You'd better put that away. Guns tend to make some folks nervous, especially lawmen. The Kansas City police ought to be here pretty soon. With all that shooting, somebody's bound to've turned in an alarm."

"Oh. Yes, of course." Schilling tucked the gun away in a small holster underneath his jacket.

Colonel Pettigrew pushed through the crowd that had gathered around Longarm, Schilling, and the dead gunman. "Kurt!" he exclaimed. "Are you all right?"

"Yes, I am fine, thank you, Jasper. This man attempted to rob me, but Marshal Long stopped him when he fled."

Pettigrew looked thunderstruck. "Tried to steal the payroll, you mean?"

"That's right."

From the expression on Pettigrew's face, Longarm knew how disastrous it would have been if the would-be robber had been successful. That might have been the final nail in the coffin of Pettigrew's show.

Longarm beat the colonel to the punch, saying quietly, "You think Trenton could've been responsible for this?"

Pettigrew's face flushed with outrage. "Damn right! I wouldn't put anything past that skunk!"

Before any of them could say anything else, a blue-uniformed Kansas City policeman came pushing through the crowd. He backed everyone off, stared in surprise for a second at the corpse, then asked harshly, "What happened here?"

Longarm told him, identifying himself to the local badge-toter as a federal lawman. "Better send for Lieutenant McClain," Longarm advised. "He's handling a case from last night that may be hooked up with this shooting."

The officer looked relieved at the suggestion. He would be more than happy to turn this matter over to a superior.

"Stay right here," he warned Longarm, Pettigrew, and Schilling. "I'll go to a callbox and get in touch with the lieutenant at headquarters."

Longarm and the other two did as they were told. More police arrived and cleared the lobby of other hotel guests and spectators who had been drawn in from the street by the commotion. While Longarm was waiting, he heard someone call, "Custis?"

He turned his head and saw Maureen Mullaney standing at the bottom of the staircase. One of the Kansas City policemen was blocking her way as she tried to come closer to Longarm. She was wearing a simple, dark green dress, and despite the relatively early hour and the fact that she hadn't gotten much sleep the night before, either, she looked fresh and lovely.

Longarm went over to her, nodding to the policeman that

it was all right. The Kansas City coppers had been advised of Longarm's status as a federal lawman, so the officer nodded and backed off. Longarm positioned himself so that he was between Maureen and the bloody corpse sprawled on the lobby floor. No need for her to see that, he told himself.

"Custis, are you all right?" Maureen asked anxiously. "I heard shooting—"

"I'm fine," Longarm assured her.

She came up on her toes and craned her neck, trying to see past him. "Is that Colonel Pettigrew and Mr. Schilling over there?"

"They're all right, too." Longarm didn't see any reason not to tell her the truth about what had happened, at least as much of it as he knew at the moment. "Some hombre tried to steal the show's payroll from Schilling, and they got into a shoot-out over it. I wound up having to ventilate the fella."

Maureen's beautiful green eyes were wide. "Is he . . . is he dead?"

"I'm afraid so."

She put her hands on his arms. "This is terrible! I can't believe such a thing could happen right here in the middle of Kansas City."

This city wasn't any more immune to violence than any other place, Longarm thought. He said quietly, "The colonel figures that Cherokee Hank was behind it."

Maureen nodded. "I'm not surprised."

"Not surprised by what? That Colonel Pettigrew thinks so, or that Trenton would do something like hire somebody to steal the payroll?"

"Either. Both." Maureen shook her head. "Oh, I don't know what I mean. What do you think, Custis?"

"I don't know . . . yet."

He was saved from the necessity of explaining that comment by the arrival of Lieutenant McClain. The detective looked tired; what with the investigation out at the arena, he probably hadn't gotten much sleep last night, either. He looked around at Longarm, Pettigrew, and Schilling and then said wearily, "You people again?" Without waiting for an answer, he went on, "Somebody tell me what happened here."

Longarm did so, with a few comments interspersed from Schilling, since the bookkeeper was the first one who had encountered the would-be payroll thief. McClain listened in silence, then grunted and asked, "Where's this payroll money now?"

"In the hotel safe, where I placed it last night," Schilling answered. "I was going to my room to prepare the pay envelopes, then I would have retrieved the money and distributed it accordingly."

McClain gestured at the dead man. "Then how did this bastard intend to get his hands on it?"

"He was going to come downstairs with me while I got the money from the safe," Schilling explained. "He told me that he would have his gun in his pocket and would be pointing it at me the entire time. He said he would kill me if I failed to cooperate."

"Did you believe him?"

"Of course I did. Had I not felt that my life was genuinely in danger, I would not have drawn my own gun and fired at him."

"You're lucky you didn't get your brains blown out," said McClain, echoing Longarm's thought of a few minutes earlier. "Ever see him before?"

One of the policemen had rolled the dead man onto his back. Longarm took a good look at him, seeing a coarse-featured, beard stubbled face that wasn't the least bit familiar. The man had a thin scar on his left cheek, probably picked up in a knife fight sometime. He was wearing range clothes—boots, jeans, a homespun shirt, and a corduroy jacket. A battered, sweat-stained Stetson had come off his head when he leaped over the second floor railing. The hat now lay a few feet from his body. Longarm looked at the man's hands and knew that he hadn't been a cowboy; no calluses on the palms from using a rope. A drifter, a small-

62

time desperado who'd tried to pull a big job. That was Longarm's assessment.

"I never saw him in my life until today," Schilling declared.

"Neither did I," Colonel Pettigrew added. "But I can tell you who put him up to tryin' to rob us."

"Let me guess," McClain said with a hint of a sneer in his voice. "Cherokee Hank Trenton."

"That's right," Pettigrew blustered. "Why don't you just go out there where he's camped and arrest him?"

"There's a little matter of evidence. I don't know that Trenton had anything to do with this, and since we can't ask this gent—" McClain nodded toward the dead man.

Pettigrew stared angrily at the detective. "You're sayin' you ain't gonna do anything about this?"

"The matter will be investigated thoroughly," McClain answered curtly. "While I'm doing that, you can go on about your business." He looked at one of the policemen standing nearby. "Go outside and see if the undertaker's wagon is here yet."

Longarm said, "If you're going to talk to Trenton, I'd like to go along."

McClain sniffed. "No offense, Marshal, but this still isn't your jurisdiction, and attempted armed robbery isn't a federal crime. Just when is it you're going back to Denver?"

"I don't rightly know," Longarm replied coolly. "But I'm the one who shot this man, Lieutenant, and I want to be sure somebody gets to the bottom of this."

"Don't worry about the shooting. I'm sure the inquest will clear you of any blame. After all, there are plenty of witnesses that this man was shooting at you first."

"Just when do you reckon the coroner will hold the inquest?"

"This afternoon, I hope. For this one and the one who got killed last night, too." McClain looked around at them. "You'll need to be there, Marshal, along with everyone from the Wild West Show."

"Blast it, we got things to do to get ready for tonight,"

63

Pettigrew objected. "We ain't got time to go to no inquest."

"Make the time," McClain advised brusquely. "Otherwise, the coroner will likely issue warrants for your arrest."

"We'll all be there," Longarm said. He gave Pettigrew a hard glance that he hoped would impress the seriousness of the situation on the showman.

"Yeah, I reckon we'll be there," Pettigrew grumbled.

The officer McClain had sent outside a few moments earlier came back into the hotel lobby and announced cheerfully, "Meat wagon's here, Lieutenant."

"Good. Get the boys in here so they can start cleaning up this mess." McClain looked at Longarm. "Stay where I can find you."

"I'll be around," Longarm promised.

It was a pledge he intended to keep. Now more than ever, he planned to stay in Kansas City until this mess was straightened out. He'd had to kill a man who'd been doing his damnedest to kill him, and that made all the difference in the world.

Now, it was personal.

Chapter 7

Lieutenant McClain left the hotel, trailed by some of the policemen who had shown up in response to the alarm. Other blue-uniformed officers stayed behind to supervise the removal of the dead gunman's body. Longarm, Maureen, Pettigrew, and Schilling went into the dining room, where they found several other members of the Wild West Show troupe waiting for them.

Lanky Asa Wilburn, the former army scout and buffalo hunter, stepped forward to meet them, a worried frown on his craggy face. "What in Hades happened a while ago?" he asked. "With all that shootin' goin' on, I thought for a minute I was back at Adobe Walls, fightin' ol' Chief Quanah and the whole damned Comanche nation."

Pettigrew jerked a thumb at Schilling. "Some no-good owlhoot tried to hold up Kurt here and steal the show's payroll."

Wilburn's eyes widened in surprise, and a hubbub of questions broke out from the other members of the group. Longarm scanned the crowd and spotted both Ben Price and Jessamine Langley. The head wrangler had his arm around the pretty trick rider, and they looked mighty cozy together. Longarm didn't see Tom Beaumont anywhere. That didn't have to mean anything, he reminded himself.

There could be all sorts of innocent reasons for Beaumont's absence.

Pettigrew went on to explain how Schilling had fought back against the would-be robber, and Wilburn smacked the bookkeeper on the back with a big hand, staggering him slightly. "Damn it, I didn't know you had that much sand," Wilburn told Schilling.

"It was Marshal Long who ultimately stopped the miscreant," Schilling pointed out. "Perhaps you should offer him your, uh, congratulations."

"Danged if I won't." Wilburn stepped over and shook Longarm's hand. "Much obliged, Marshal."

"*De nada*," Longarm said. "It ain't like the gent ever got his hands on the money. It was locked up tight in the hotel safe all along."

"Well, you made sure that son of a bitch won't ever try to rob nobody else, didn't you?"

Longarm inclined his head in acknowledgment of Wilburn's point. It was true the hold-up man would never try the same stunt again.

Still and all, Longarm couldn't help but wish he'd been able to bring the man down without killing him. If he and McClain had been able to question the robber, it might have cleared up some things.

Well, he'd just have to go about it the long way, he told himself. He said to Pettigrew, "You folks had better stick pretty close to the hotel this morning, in case Lieutenant McClain wants to find you."

"How about you?" Pettigrew asked. "What do you intend to do, Marshal?"

"Thought I'd go have a talk with Trenton," Longarm said.

Pettigrew frowned. "That lieutenant feller pretty much told you not to do that."

"He said it wasn't my jurisdiction," Longarm replied, "but he didn't order me not to."

"No, I reckon he didn't." Pettigrew was solemn as he added, "But I like you, Marshal. You better be careful if you go out yonder to where Trenton's camped. He's liable to try anything, and I wouldn't want to see you hurt on our account."

"It's not just on your account," Longarm said, but he didn't explain how he had come to feel about this case. That was his own business.

He left The Cattlemen's Hotel and decided to go in search of a livery stable. If he was going to be staying around Kansas City for a while, he needed to rent a horse and a saddle. Eventually, when he got back to Denver and turned in his expense vouchers, Billy Vail might disallow them since they weren't directly connected to a federal investigation, but Longarm couldn't do anything about that. He wasn't going to tramp all over the city on foot.

Before locating a livery stable, however, he stopped back by the Western Union office. The same operator was still on duty. He looked up, saw Longarm, and said, "Got a reply to your wire, Marshal." He came to the counter and handed a yellow telegraph flimsy to Longarm.

The message was too short to contain the background information he had requested on Pettigrew and Trenton, Longarm saw at a glance. ASSIST BIA ANYWAY POSSIBLE STOP, the block printing read. WORKING ON REQUEST STOP EXPECT SEE YOU IN DENVER SOON STOP VAIL.

Billy was telling him not to lollygag around once his chore for the Bureau of Indian Affairs was finished, Longarm knew. As soon as he was contacted by Katherine Nash again so he could explain to her that Princess Little Feather wasn't Chief Lame Bear's long-lost daughter, Longarm's job here would be over. Vail would expect Longarm to catch the first train after that.

After all these years, though, you'd think that Billy would understand he wasn't one to always go strictly by the book, Longarm told himself with a faint smile.

"There'll probably be another wire coming in later," Longarm told the operator. He gave the man the name of the hotel where he was staying. "I'll either be there or at The Cattlemen's Hotel, more than likely."

The operator nodded. "I'll send a boy to find you if anything comes in, Marshal."

Longarm slid a silver dollar across the counter and started to leave the office, then stopped and looked back. "There a good livery stable around here?"

"Rickert's," the operator answered. "Three blocks west, then two north."

"Much obliged."

The place turned out to be a combination of livery stable and wagon yard, with a large barn, several good-sized corrals out back, and a big open lot covered with wagons. Longarm dealt with the owner himself, a jovial sort who was only too happy to rent a chestnut mare and a saddle to the big lawman.

"Best riding mount I've got," Rickert said as he patted the animal on the flank while Longarm handled the saddling himself. "You'll take good care of her?"

"You got my word on it," Longarm said. He pulled the cinches tight. The saddle was a double-cinched cowboy's rig. Longarm preferred his old McClellan, but this would do in a pinch. He'd already paid for a couple of days' rental, so he put his left foot in the stirrup and stepped up into the saddle, swinging his right leg over the horse's back.

As he did so, something caught his eye. A poster was tacked up on the wall of Rickert's barn that faced the street. Longarm walked the horse over to it so that he could read the poster.

CHEROKEE HANK'S FABULOUS WILD WEST SHOW AND CIRCUS! SEE THE WILD WEST COME TO LIFE! SAVAGE INDIANS! EXOTIC ANIMALS! THRILLS THRILLS THRILLS!

The garish drawings that accompanied the words reminded Longarm of the advertising flier Katherine Nash had shown him. Cherokee Hank didn't have trick riders or sharpshooters on his poster, however. Instead, he had lions and tigers, along with a scene of Indians battling cavalry troopers.

That was because Trenton's outfit had started out as a

circus, Longarm reminded himself. That explained the wild animals.

Rickert walked up beside him. "Thinking about going to the Wild West Show, Marshal? Hear there's another one in town, too."

Longarm pointed at the poster. "You know where this one's being held?" he asked.

"Grant's meadow," Rickert replied. "They have horse races out there sometimes, too. Take the river road north. You'll see it on your right about a mile out of town."

"Thanks," Longarm said. He turned the horse, heeled it into an easy trot.

He didn't have any trouble finding the river road. The Missouri was wide and brown and slow-moving, living up to its nickname of the Big Muddy. The road followed the river's gentle bends, and Longarm enjoyed the ride. The morning was well along now, with the sun high in the sky casting spring warmth over the prairie.

After only a short time, he spotted the huge, red-and-white striped canvas structure that rose from an open field on the right side of the road. As he rode closer, he saw the wagons parked around the big tent and people moving here and there in a flurry of activity. Getting ready for the show tonight, Longarm thought.

Depending on what happened when he talked to Cherokee Hank Trenton, there might not *be* a show tonight.

He stopped the first man he came to, a burly gent with shirtsleeves rolled up on brawny forearms and a shapeless hat mashed down on his head. "Where can I find Cherokee Hank?" Longarm asked the man.

"Who wants to know?" the man shot back, a little belligerently.

"A U.S. deputy marshal," Longarm replied, letting an edge creep into his voice.

"Oh. Well, in that case . . ." The man jerked a thumb toward one of the vehicles. "That's the headquarters wagon. You should probably try it first. If the boss ain't there, he's around somewhere. Just keep asking."

"Obliged," Longarm said. He rode over to the wagon the man had indicated and swung down from the saddle.

The wagon's team had been unhitched and put into a corral somewhere, Longarm supposed. He looped his mount's reins around the brake lever and then stepped to the rear of the wagon, where a door was built into the wooden covering over the bed. The wagon reminded him a little of a gypsy wagon, or one from a medicine show, only it wasn't painted garish colors and didn't have any fancy writing on it. It was plain, utilitarian.

Longarm rapped his knuckles on the closed door. For a moment there was no response and he was about to decide that Trenton wasn't here, but then the door swung open and a small, wizened face peered out at him. "Yes?" asked a mild voice with a trace of a southern accent. "Can I help you, sir?"

"I'm looking for the boss of this outfit," Longarm said. "A fella named Henry Trenton, calls himself Cherokee Hank."

The man came out of the wagon, using a pair of wooden steps to climb down to the ground. "I'm Cherokee Hank," he announced. "What can I do for you?"

Longarm had a difficult time not staring in surprise at the man. After hearing everything Colonel Pettigrew had to say about Cherokee Hank, Longarm had halfway expected the rival Wild West Show owner to be some sort of fire-breathing giant. Instead, Longarm found himself looking at a slender, middle-aged man a head shorter than himself, with wispy fair hair, guileless blue eyes, and open, friendly features. The man was dressed in a brown tweed suit.

"*You're* Cherokee Hank?" Longarm couldn't stop the exclamation from escaping.

"That's right." Trenton smiled. "I'm afraid you have the advantage of me, sir."

"Long, Custis Long. United States deputy marshal."

Trenton's eyes widened, and the smile on his face slipped a little. "Oh, my," he said. "Is this an official visit, Marshal?"

"I'm afraid so," Longarm said. "There's been some trouble in Kansas City—"

"Trouble with Colonel Pettigrew's show, I'll wager," Trenton cut in. "And he says that I'm to blame for all of it."

From the sound of the comments, Lieutenant McClain hadn't been out here yet to question Trenton. That came as a bit of a surprise to Longarm, but he didn't mind taking advantage of the opportunity to poke around first.

"Sounds like you've heard this before."

"Oh, yes," Trenton said with a sigh. "No matter what goes wrong, Jasper screams to high heaven that I'm responsible for it. First it was those missing costumes, then some of their saddles, and the hotel reservations . . . What's happened now, Marshal? I'm surprised it's something serious enough to warrant federal intervention."

"Two men are dead," Longarm said grimly.

Trenton's smile disappeared completely at that. "Dead?" he repeated, a squeak in his voice.

"That's right."

"I promise you, Marshal, I had nothing to do with whatever caused this . . . this terrible tragedy! Jasper and I are competitors, yes, but I've always tried to treat him fairly. To be honest, in the past his antics and accusations have been rather amusing as well as annoying at times, but surely he doesn't really believe that I would . . . that I could have anything to do with—"

Longarm stopped the stream of words tumbling out of Trenton's mouth by saying, "Where were you last night after Pettigrew's show was over?"

"Why, out here at our camp, of course. We just arrived late yesterday afternoon, and we were already busy setting up for the first show tonight." Trenton put a hand on his chest. "You're accusing *me*? Me personally? Of killing two men?"

"You didn't kill the second one," Longarm said, without explaining who actually had fired the fatal shot. "I reckon some of your folks can vouch for you being here?"

71

"Of course!"

"What about the rest of them? Did anybody from your show leave this camp last night?"

"Well, I don't actually know. I doubt it, everyone was busy, but I couldn't say with any degree of certainty . . . Marshal, you simply can't believe that I or any of my people would stoop to murder to harm Colonel Pettigrew's show!"

To tell the truth, it was hard to look at Henry Trenton and think that he would ever hurt anything, even a fly. But Longarm had encountered mousy little sorts just like him in the past who had turned out to be cold-blooded killers. At this stage of the game, he wasn't going to rule out anybody.

"I'm going to talk to some of your folks," Longarm said. "I ain't asking permission, just letting you know."

"By all means. Question anyone you like, Marshal. You won't find the guilty party here, I assure you of that."

Longarm indulged his curiosity. "Where'd you come up with the name Cherokee Hank?"

Trenton squared his narrow shoulders and lifted his head proudly. "It's part of my heritage. I'm part Cherokee, you know."

Trenton looked about as much like an Indian as Longarm looked like an Eskimo. His disbelief must have showed on his face, because Trenton went on, "I'm from Georgia, and many of the Cherokees lived there before they were removed to Indian Territory. I don't know if you're aware of that or not—"

"I've heard of the Trail of Tears," Longarm said.

"Well, that's where our ancestry intermingled, there in Georgia. I'm one-sixty-fourth Cherokee, which entitles me to declare myself part of the Cherokee Nation."

And it made for a good name to go on posters and advertising fliers, Longarm thought. He wondered what sort of costume Trenton wore in the Wild West Show. A bluff, hearty sort like Colonel Pettigrew could wear a buckskin jacket and a big white Stetson and look like a Westerner.

Longarm couldn't quite see Trenton carrying that off. He decided that he would try to watch Trenton's show before he headed back to Denver, if he had the chance.

Longarm inclined his head toward the bustle of activity around them. "You want to introduce me to some of your people, or do I just start asking questions?"

Trenton sighed again and said, "You'll get a much better reception if I accompany you. Come along, Marshal."

They started strolling toward the big tent, and Longarm figured they probably made sort of a funny-looking pair, what with him being so much taller than Trenton. Before they reached the tent, Trenton called to one of the men who was hurrying by. "Calvin! A moment of your time, please."

The man stopped and turned. "Yeah, boss?"

Trenton said, "Marshal, this is Calvin Strang. He's my second-in-command, so to speak, and actually runs the day-to-day operation of the show. Calvin, this is Marshal . . . Long, was it?"

"Custis Long," Longarm said. He didn't offer to shake hands and neither did Strang.

"What's a lawman want with us?" Strang asked. His lip curled a little. "You ain't one of these local yokels always coming around with his hand out for a bribe, are you, Long? Show people run into that kind all the time."

Longarm kept a rein on his temper. Strang struck him as a surly sort to begin with. The man was as tall as Longarm, broad-shouldered and thick-bodied. He had a heavy jaw, and his head was bald as an egg.

"I'm a U.S. marshal, not local," Longarm said, "but I'm looking into a local matter right now. There's been some trouble at Colonel Pettigrew's Wild West Show."

Strang's mouth twisted into an outright sneer. He leaned over and spat on the ground. "*Colonel Pettigrew*'s a damned fraud. He ain't no more a colonel than I am. What's he complaining about now?"

"Please, Calvin," Trenton said. "According to the marshal here, a couple of men have died."

Strang's brow furrowed. "Died how?" he demanded.

73

"There was a stampede last night after the show was over," Longarm said. "One of the wranglers was trampled, a fella named Alf Culpepper."

Trenton shook his head and murmured, "How terrible."

"You don't think any of us had anything to do with that stampede, do you, Marshal?" Strang challenged.

"Well, I don't rightly know. That's why I'm here asking questions."

Strang's big hands balled into fists. "Damn it, our show's twice as good as Pettigrew's! We don't have to resort to dirty tricks and killing people to take business away from him."

From the looks of it, Trenton's operation was on stronger financial ground than Pettigrew's, Longarm thought. Admittedly, he hadn't seen much of it yet, but the big tent was well-kept and several of the wagons had fresh coats of paint on them.

"What about the second man who died?" Trenton asked. "Was that an accident, too?"

"If that stampede was started deliberately, then Culpepper's death was murder," Longarm pointed out. "As for the second fella, he came to a bad end this morning—while he was trying to hold up Pettigrew's bookkeeper and steal the show's payroll."

Strang took a step toward him. "So now you're accusing us of being thieves as well as killers!"

"I said the hombre *tried* to steal the payroll," Longarm replied coolly. "He never got his hands on the money before I had to ventilate him."

"Sounds to me like you're the only killer around here, Marshal," Strang said.

Longarm had had enough. He said, "I want to talk to everybody connected with this outfit. I want to know where they were last night, and where they were this morning—"

"Go to hell," Strang snapped.

And with that, he swung a knobby-knuckled fist right at Longarm's head.

Chapter 8

Longarm saw the blow coming and had no trouble ducking under it as Trenton yelped, "Calvin! Don't—"

Strang wasn't in any mood to listen to reason. He quickly recovered his balance after missing the roundhouse swing and came bulling at Longarm, trying to envelope him in a bear hug. Judging by the width of Strang's shoulders and the way his muscles bulged his shirt, if he was able to get Longarm in his grip he might be capable of crushing the lawman's ribs.

Longarm didn't want that. He stepped inside and slammed a hard right and left combination into Strang's midsection. It was almost like punching a plank wall, but the blows had enough of an effect to slow Strang's lunge. He tried to close his arms around Longarm, but instead he got a sharp left uppercut to the jaw that rocked his head back.

Longarm didn't much like bare-knuckle brawling. It was too easy to break a knuckle or some other bone, and a man in his line of work couldn't risk injuring his gun hand. He used his right to send another shot to Strang's body, this time catching the man in the solar plexus. Strang bent forward, some of the breath knocked out of him.

Not all of it, though, because he was able to let out a

yell as he stumbled back a step. Quite a few of the men who were working to prepare for that night's show had already noticed the scuffle, and at Strang's shout, they came running toward the two combatants. Longarm had no doubt whose side they would take in the battle.

Trenton waved his arm and shouted, "No! No fighting!" The men ignored him, caught up as they were in the emotion of the moment as they hurried to defend one of their own.

Facing odds like this, Longarm knew the smart thing to do would be to draw his gun and fire off a couple of rounds into the sky. Gunshots had a way of getting the attention of just about anybody, no matter how worked up they were. But he was still angry, and the frustration of the past few days boiled up in him. He kept his fists clenched and set his feet, ready to take on however many of the Wild West Show workers wanted to jump him.

The first man to reach Longarm swung a wild blow that missed so badly Longarm didn't even have to dodge it. He crouched and jolted a solid left to the sternum that stopped the man like running into a brick wall. The fella's face turned white, then red as he gasped for breath. One of the men running up behind him shoved him aside and dived at Longarm.

Neatly avoiding the tackle, Longarm stepped instead into a punch from another man that grazed the side of his head. The raking impact was enough to make him grunt in pain, and he was glad the blow hadn't landed a little lower. It might have torn his ear off if it had.

Longarm counterpunched, a right to the belly, a left cross to the head. His opponent twisted and went to a knee, to be immediately replaced by another of Strang's cronies. This man got a right fist past Longarm's guard and planted it in his midsection. Longarm stumbled back a couple of steps, fighting off the sickness that tried to well up inside him. He caught his balance as his latest opponent bored in, intent on seizing the momentary advantage.

To the man's surprise, he was met by a flurry of blows

76

that staggered him. In the heat of the moment, Longarm forgot about protecting his right and threw a punch with that hand that slammed into the man's jaw and lifted him off the ground. The man landed on his back, crumpling into a heap, knocked senseless and out of the fight.

Longarm didn't have time to savor that small triumph. Suddenly, strong hands grabbed him from behind, clamping painful grips on his arms and pinning them to his sides. He thrashed wildly but was unable to dislodge the men who held him. Calvin Strang came at him from the front, both fists poised to strike. "I'm gonna beat the hell out of you, mister," Strang snarled.

As soon as Strang was close enough, Longarm kicked him in the balls.

With the men ganging up on him like this, he was damned if he was going to worry about fighting fair. He sank the toe of his boot in Strang's groin and felt a surge of exultation as he saw Strang turn as pale as a sheet. Strang howled in agony and clutched himself, then toppled onto the ground like a falling tree.

"You son of a bitch!" grated one of the men holding Longarm. "We'll kill you for that!"

Longarm doubted that, but he figured he was in for a bad beating unless he could get his hand on his gun. Burning off some of his accumulated frustration was one thing; getting all busted up was another.

But he didn't have to try to reach his Colt, because someone else fired a pair of shots. The wicked cracking of a handgun made the angry men gathered around Longarm freeze.

"Let go of him!" a familiar female voice ordered.

Longarm twisted his head. At first he couldn't see her, but then a gap opened in the circle of men. The hands fell away from the big lawman's arms, and he saw Maureen Mullaney striding toward him, brandishing six-guns in both hands.

"I'll shoot the ears off the next man who throws a

punch," she said furiously. "You've likely seen me shoot. You know I can do it!"

She wasn't dressed as Princess Little Feather at the moment. Instead of the buckskin dress, dark makeup, and black wig, she wore boots, a brown riding skirt, and a white shirt with a cowhide vest over it. A white Stetson sat on her thick red hair, its strap tight under her chin. She reminded Longarm of a dude Eastern gal playing cowgirl, but at the moment she was a damned welcome sight.

Especially considering that she had a gun belt with double-hung buscadero holsters strapped around her trim hips and those ivory-handled Colts in each hand.

Trenton's men backed away from Longarm. The diminutive Wild West Show owner hustled up to Longarm and said, "I'm sorry, Marshal. I didn't mean for this to happen, I swear I didn't—"

Longarm ignored Trenton and said to Maureen, "What are you doing out here?"

"The more I thought about it, the more worried I got about you coming out here by yourself," she replied. "So I went to the arena and got one of the horses and rode out after you."

"You must've ridden fast to have gotten here so quick."

She smiled. "I didn't want anything to happen to you, Custis."

Remembering how they had made love the night before, Longarm knew what she meant. He wouldn't have wanted anything bad to befall her, either.

"Marshal," Trenton said insistently. "Marshal, this unfortunate incident isn't going to have any legal repercussions, is it?"

Longarm frowned at him. "You mean like me shutting down your show, Trenton?"

A new voice said, "I don't think that's going to happen."

Longarm knew this voice, too, but it wasn't nearly as welcome as Maureen Mullaney's had been a few minutes earlier. He turned his head and saw Lieutenant McClain striding toward him, followed by a couple of blue-uniformed Kansas City coppers.

McClain came to a stop, put his hands on his hips, and glared at Longarm. "What are you doing out here?"

"No law against paying a visit to a Wild West Show, is there, Lieutenant?" Longarm replied coolly.

Trenton looked back and forth between Longarm and McClain for a few seconds, then said, "You mean this man *isn't* here as a duly authorized representative of the law?"

"Uncle Sam's law," McClain rasped. "Who're you?"

Trenton drew himself up to his full height. "Cherokee Hank Trenton," he announced proudly.

"Just the man I wanted to see," McClain said. "If you haven't broken any federal statutes, Mr. Trenton, then Marshal Long doesn't have any business with you."

Trenton cast a triumphant glance at Longarm. "I'm a law-abiding man—federal, state, and local."

"That's what I'm here to determine." McClain looked at Longarm and Maureen. "You two can go."

Longarm's eyes narrowed. "You mean assault ain't a crime in Kansas City? These men jumped me and tried to whale the tar out of me."

A humorless smile stretched McClain's thin lips. "I'll look into the matter," he said, but Longarm didn't believe him for a second. "In the meantime, I've got more pressing questions to ask."

Trenton said, "We'll be glad to cooperate, Mr.—?"

"It's Lieutenant, Lieutenant McClain of the Kansas City Police."

"If this is about the unfortunate incidents concerning Colonel Jasper Pettigrew's Wild West Show, I assure you, Lieutenant, neither I nor any of my employees had anything to do with them."

McClain gave Longarm a withering glance. "You told them all about it, did you?"

"Just asked a few questions," Longarm said.

"I'll say it plainer," McClain snapped. "Both of you move along. Stay out of this investigation, Marshal. It's a local matter, and if you keep interfering, I'm going to send a wire of complaint to the Justice Department."

That would bring Billy Vail down on him like a rockslide, Longarm knew. But Vail had chewed his ass up one way and down the other many times in the past, and Longarm was still around, still doing his job as he saw fit. If Vail gave him a direct order to return to Denver, however, Longarm would have to think long and hard before he would disregard it. A fella who liked to bend the rules, as he had done on occasion, had to be careful not to turn into an out-and-out renegade.

"We're going," Longarm said tightly. He took Maureen's arm. "Come on."

The crowd had closed back in a little. It parted again as Longarm and Maureen walked toward the headquarters wagon. He saw another horse tied to the wagon beside the one he had rented back in Kansas City and figured it was Maureen's mount.

"Reckon I'd better say I'm much obliged for the way you gave me a hand," he told her as they walked over to the horses. "I ain't no pantywaist when it comes to fighting, but those boys would've thrashed me, sure as hell. There were just too many of 'em."

"I know," she said. "That's why I thought I'd better get their attention by firing off a couple of blanks."

Longarm stopped and looked at her. "Blanks?"

"I'm afraid so. I use a mixture of blanks and live ammunition in my performances. Some of the tricks are just that—tricks. I'm a good shot, but some things are physically impossible."

"Blanks?" Longarm said again.

"Of course. I didn't want to actually *hurt* anybody. I just wanted to scare them into leaving you alone."

"Well, you did that," he admitted as he untied his horse. "Next time you go facing down an angry mob, though, it might be a good idea to have real bullets in your guns."

"I don't intend for there to be a next time."

Longarm agreed with that. In his experience, though, when it came to trouble there was *always* a next time.

On the ride back into Kansas City, Longarm found himself enjoying Maureen's company but discouraged by the fact that his visit to Trenton's camp hadn't really accomplished anything except to get him some bruises. Trenton had denied having anything to do with Colonel Pettigrew's troubles, and while it was true that he didn't seem the type to resort to sabotage, nor did the success of his operation mean that he would need to, Longarm knew that wasn't proof of anything.

Still, on the face of it, it was just as likely that the stampede that had taken Alf Culpepper's life could have been an accident. If it wasn't, then Tom Beaumont was just as likely a suspect as someone working for Trenton. Jealousy over a woman had probably produced more murders over the years than business rivalries, Longarm mused.

And as for the robbery attempt that morning, hell, anybody could have decided to try to steal the show's payroll. Such a crime didn't have to be connected to anything else. Most of the time, the simplest answer was also the right one, Longarm had learned.

Then why was his backbone still so itchy, as if a gunman had a bead on him right now?

Maureen asked, "Are you paying attention to a word I'm saying, Custis?"

He gave a little shake as her question pulled him out of his reverie. "Of course I'm paying attention," he replied, trying to sound a little indignant that she would even ask such a thing.

"Then what did I just say to you?"

Longarm grimaced as he tried to recall the words. "Hell," he muttered after a moment.

"I thought so," Maureen said smugly, but her grin took any real sting out of the words. "For all you know, I could have been saying that I can't wait until we're alone together again and buck naked and you've got that big thing of

81

yours stuck way up inside me as far as it'll go . . ."

Longarm swallowed hard and said, "I'm listening."

Maureen took a deep breath. She was a little flushed. The day was warm, but not *that* warm. "Just keep that in mind when I'm talking to you," she said.

"Yes, ma'am. I will." Longarm fished a cheroot out of his vest pocket and took an educated guess. "As for what you were saying before that, I reckon you must've been talking about the trouble between Cherokee Hank and Colonel Pettigrew."

"Cherokee Hank," she repeated disdainfully. "Did you ever see a man with such an ill-suited name?"

Longarm scratched a lucifer into life and held the flame to the tip of his cheroot. When he had the smoke going, he said, "Trenton don't look much like a Cherokee to me, but I reckon he could be. He only claims to be one-sixty-fourth Indian."

"He only claims that for his show."

"Like Colonel Pettigrew claims to be a colonel?" Maybe she wouldn't mind talking about some of her fellow members of the troupe, he thought.

"He *was* a colonel," Maureen insisted.

"In whose army?"

She hesitated. "The Connecticut militia."

Longarm tried not to grin. "So he's not really a frontiersman?"

"I didn't say that. He's been all over the West."

"In a medicine show?" Longarm guessed.

Maureen's silence told him that his speculation was right. After a moment, she said, "There's nothing wrong with being an entertainer."

"Nope. I've met Miss Sarah Bernhardt and Miss Lily Langtry both. Fine gals."

Maureen looked over at him as she kept her horse at a steady walk. "How in the world did you meet such famous actresses?" she asked.

Longarm put the cheroot in his mouth and cocked it at a jaunty angle between his teeth. Around it, he said, "I may be an old country boy from West-by-God Virginia, but I get around."

Maureen laughed. "I'll bet you do, Custis. I'll just bet you do!"

After a moment, he went on, "How'd you hook up with the colonel, anyway?"

"I joined the show in New York. I was born and raised there. That's where I learned to shoot. My father took me hunting ever since I was a little girl. He said I had a better eye than any of my brothers."

"That explains how come you can handle a rifle. Where'd you learn to use a six-gun?"

"It's just something I came by naturally. A few years ago, a man I was seeing let me use his pistol for some target practice. I saw right away how to point and shoot."

"What happened to that fella?"

Maureen laughed. "He decided he wasn't romantically interested in a woman who could shoot coins out of the air. To tell the truth, I think he was a little frightened of me."

Longarm could see how that might happen, all right. With the exception of his old friend Jessie Starbuck from down Texas way, he had never run into a woman who could come close to shooting as well as he did. He was struck suddenly by an impulse.

Reining the horse to a stop, he pointed into a field on the opposite side of the road from the Missouri River. "See that little dead tree about fifty feet out in the field?" he asked.

Maureen had brought her own mount to a stop beside him. She nodded and said, "I see it."

"Reckon you could hit that top branch from here?"

"I told you," she said, "my guns have blanks in them."

He slipped his Colt out and offered it to her, butt-first. "Use mine. Or I've got spare cartridges, if you want to reload one of your own guns."

Maureen looked at him for a long moment, eyes narrowed. "What is this?" she finally asked. "Is your male

83

pride threatened by the idea that I might be able to outshoot you, Custis?"

"Nope," he said honestly. "I'm just curious. Besides, you never know when you might have to side my play again. I like to know the person watching my back can handle themselves, whether it's a gent or a gal."

"Oh, all right," she said. "Give me the gun."

She took the Colt from him and then dismounted, handing him the reins to hold. Stepping to the edge of the road, she raised her arm until the pistol was held out level in front of her. She aimed carefully, then squeezed the trigger.

The gun cracked. Longarm wasn't sure where the bullet went, but the branch angling out just below the top of the dead tree didn't move. Maureen looked back over her shoulder at him and said, "I have to get used to the gun."

"Uh-huh," Longarm said.

She made a face at him, then lined up her second shot. This time when the gun blasted, the last six inches or so of the branch went flying into the air, sheered cleanly off the rest of the branch by the bullet. While Longarm's eyes were still widening at that, the Colt boomed twice more. The rest of the branch was blown off the tree next to the trunk, and the upper part of the trunk itself sagged to the side where Maureen's third bullet had blasted part of it away.

Longarm let out a low whistle of admiration. "That's damned fine shooting," he said.

Maureen turned toward him and reversed the gun. She held up to him. "Satisfied?"

Longarm took the gun, reloaded the empty chambers except for the one on which the hammer rested, and slipped it back into its holster. "I still haven't seen you shoot coins out of the air," he said dryly.

"I haven't seen you do that, either," she pointed out.

Longarm looked toward a line of trees on the far side of the field, maybe two hundred yards away. "Looks like there's a creek over there," he said. "Come on."

"You mean it?"

"Sure."

With a smile, Maureen swung up into her saddle and then rode alongside him across the field. They reached the trees, and just as Longarm had predicted, there was a small creek running through them. They followed the stream to a clearing, where Longarm reined in and dismounted.

"Why did you want to come over here?" Maureen asked as she followed his example.

Longarm grinned. "So nobody else will see me if I make a fool of myself," he answered honestly.

"All right." Maureen reached in the pocket of her riding skirt and came up with a silver dollar. "Will this do?"

"I reckon," Longarm said. He stepped off several paces to the side and pushed back his coat, giving him free access to the Colt in the crossdraw rig. A part of him couldn't believe he was actually doing this. Showing off with a gun went against the grain for him. It was something a wet-behind-the-ears kid with visions of gunfighter glory would do. To Longarm, a gun had always been a tool, one of the instruments that allowed him to do his job and often saved his life. This was sheer foolishness.

But as he looked at Maureen, he knew he had to do it anyway.

She had the coin poised in her hand. "You tell me when," she said.

Longarm took a breath, held it, released it. "Now," he said.

Maureen sent the silver dollar spinning high into the air. Longarm's right hand flashed across to the left side of his body and palmed out the Colt. As his eyes tracked the spinning coin, he realized he had made a mistake by coming here into the trees. Sure, it was more discreet, but the background was no good, and the alternating patterns of shadow and light made the coin even harder to see. Still, he had gone too far to back out now. He allowed instinct to take over as the gun in his hand came up.

One, two, three, four times the Colt blasted. The first three times, the silver dollar leaped in the air, thrown high by the bullets striking it. The fourth shot was a clean miss,

Longarm realized as the coin dropped back to earth with a soft thud. "Damn," he said quietly as he lowered the gun and turned to look at Maureen.

She was staring wide-eyed at him.

"What's the matter?" Longarm asked. "I know I missed that last shot—"

"But you hit the first three," she said, amazement in her voice. "You hit the coin in mid-air three times."

"Yeah, I reckon, but I missed—"

"How often do you practice that trick?"

"Trick?" Longarm repeated with a frown. "There's no trick to it. I just look at what I'm shooting at—"

Again she interrupted him. "That's the most incredible shooting I've ever seen."

"Well, you were pretty good yourself," he said.

Maureen came toward him. "Put that gun away," she said huskily.

Longarm holstered the Colt and said, "What's the matter?"

"Nothing," she said as she came into his arms. "Not a thing."

Then her mouth reached up for his.

The hot, urgent kiss lasted for a long moment. Longarm felt himself growing hard with need. Maureen reached down, found the bulge of his manhood, and caressed it through his trousers. Longarm's embrace grew tighter. He slid his arms down to her hips and cupped the gentle swells of her buttocks.

Maureen's fingers flew over the buttons of his trousers, deftly unfastening them and freeing his shaft. As her fingers closed around it, she sighed, deep in her throat. She broke the kiss and whispered, "I want to taste you this time."

Slowly, she went to her knees before him on the soft grass of the creek bank. She loosened the chin strap of her hat and pushed it back so that it dangled behind her. She leaned closer to his manhood, so close that Longarm could feel the warmth of her breath on the rigid pole.

Maureen let out a soft moan as she grasped him with

86

both hands and rubbed the velvety skin of the shaft's head over her face. Her tongue darted out, flicking against him in short, sharp, maddening blows. She trailed kisses down each side of the shaft in turn.

Longarm's pulse hammered in his head, and his heart thudded heavily in his chest. He was already aroused almost to the breaking point. He rested his hands on Maureen's shoulders as she opened her mouth wide and leaned closer to him. Her lips engulfed him.

Longarm closed his eyes, reveling in the sensations as Maureen began to suck on his stalk. She was damned fluent in French, he soon realized. He was so well-endowed that she couldn't take near all of it in her mouth, but she was plenty enthusiastic about what she *could* get in. Her tongue swirled around the head, wetting it thoroughly.

For several minutes, her oral caresses brought him higher and higher. When she took her mouth away from him, he almost let out a yell like a scalded panther. "Give me everything you have, Custis," she pleaded. "I want it."

So did Longarm. When she went back to what she had been doing, he shifted his hands from her shoulders to her head, burying his fingers in the thick red strands of her hair. He couldn't hold back any longer, and he hoped she knew that.

His climax seized him. His seed began to spurt, and Maureen's throat muscles worked as she swallowed all she could. Longarm let out a long sigh of release as the explosions shuddered through him.

When he was finally done and his shaft had slipped out from between her lips, Maureen gave the tip of it one last kiss. Then she looked up at Longarm with a smile. "I'll say one thing for you, Custis," she declared. "You shoot better than anybody I've ever seen."

Longarm wasn't quite sure how to take that, but he figured either way was a compliment.

Chapter 9

What with one thing and another, it was midday by the time Longarm and Maureen got back to The Cattlemen's Hotel. As far as Longarm knew, the inquests into the deaths of Alf Culpepper and the unknown gunman from that morning were to be held during the afternoon, so after having lunch with Maureen in the hotel dining room, he headed for the Western Union office again. While he had the chance, he wanted to see if Billy Vail had sent him another wire.

A different operator was on duty at the key. When Longarm identified himself, the man said, "Oh, yes, Marshal Long. A wire just came in for you. I saw the note from Lester saying that I was to have a boy come and find you. I was just about to do that."

"I been out of pocket anyway," Longarm said. "I'll take the wire now."

The operator passed a telegraph form filled with the usual block printing across the counter. Longarm's eyes scanned the message from Billy Vail. It mentioned Jasper Pettigrew's service in the Connecticut militia and his background as a medicine show performer—as well as a couple of arrests for fraud. No convictions, though, Longarm noted. Those brushes with the law probably stemmed from whatever snake oil Pettigrew had been selling at the time. Some folks tended to get a mite upset when they discovered that the cure-all elixir really didn't cure anything except the seller's empty pockets.

Henry Trenton, too, had been in a few scrapes, most notably several charges of theft which had to do with non-payment of rent. All of those charges were well over a decade old, however.

So Pettigrew had gotten in trouble with his medicine show and Trenton had skipped out on some landlords, Longarm mused. Neither offense was anything terribly incriminating, and certainly they didn't indicate a tendency toward more serious crime. In other words, Longarm thought, he had learned a little more about both men, but what he'd learned didn't amount to a hill of beans.

Longarm folded the telegram and put it in his pocket. "Much obliged," he nodded to the Western Union operator.

"You want me to send a boy to find you if I get any more messages for you, Marshal?"

"I'm not expecting any, but sure, if one comes in that'll be fine."

Longarm left the telegraph office and returned to the hotel, running into Colonel Pettigrew, Kurt Schilling, and Asa Wilburn in the lobby.

"A policeman came by a few minutes ago," Pettigrew told Longarm. "Said we was to be at the courthouse at two o'clock for those inquests."

Longarm nodded and took out his Ingersoll watch, flipping it open to check the time. It was one-fifteen.

"Forty-five minutes from now," he said as he closed the turnip and put it away. "Time enough for a drink."

Wilburn slapped him on the shoulder. "I like the way this hombre thinks!"

The four men went into the bar, Schilling somewhat reluctantly. He was still a little pale, and Longarm wondered if the morning's shooting was still bothering him.

They took a table, and Wilburn signaled to the bartender for a bottle and glasses. Longarm stretched out his legs and crossed them at the ankles. He looked at Schilling and said, "I hear tell you used to be a professor."

Schilling nodded. "That is correct. I taught mathematics at the University of Heidelberg. Have you heard of it?"

"Seems like I have," Longarm said. Something suddenly occurred to him, a connection that he dredged up out of his memory and briefly considered. It was so far-fetched, though, that he discarded it almost immediately.

"I suppose you wonder how an academic such as myself finds himself working in an American Wild West Show."

Longarm had wondered that, all right, and since Schilling had brought it up, he admitted, "Yep, that crossed my mind."

Before Schilling could elaborate, the bartender arrived with a bottle of whiskey and glasses on a tray. The next few moments were concerned with pouring drinks, and then Colonel Pettigrew lifted his glass. "To Lady Luck," he said. "We sure could use a visit from her."

The others echoed the toast. "To Lady Luck!" Longarm threw back his drink. For bar whiskey, it wasn't bad, certainly not as vile as the strychnine-laced, bathtub-brewed Who-hit-John he'd imbibed in many a frontier saloon. But this was Kansas City—civilization—so what else could he expect?

Kurt Schilling sipped from his glass, licked his lips, then said, "I have long had a fascination with your country, especially your western frontier. Your dime novels are very popular in Europe, you know."

Longarm shook his head. "Nope, I didn't know that." He enjoyed reading, but he tended to avoid the yellow-backed yarns of Deadwood Dick and the like. Too many of them, he had discovered, were written by Eastern scribblers with no knowledge of what the West was really like.

"Indeed. So when I found myself facing a, ah, personal crisis, I decided to come see the American wilderness for myself." Schilling drank again, this time downing most of the liquor remaining in his glass.

Pettigrew splashed more whiskey in his glass, then said,

90

"I ain't one to pry, Kurt, but this personal problem of yours, did it involve a woman?"

"Always does, don't it?" drawled Wilburn.

Schilling nodded. "Yes. A *fraulein*. The loveliest woman I have ever seen." He put away the rest of his drink and reached for the bottle.

"Unfortunately, she chose another over me. I could not bear to remain in my homeland, knowing that she was married to another man."

Longarm shook his head. "A sad story, but I reckon not an uncommon one."

Pettigrew finished his second drink, then said, "We've all been done wrong, gents, at one time or other. It's just second nature for a gal to tear out a feller's heart and stomp on it."

Wilburn and Schilling both nodded in agreement. Longarm sipped his drink. He'd been young and foolish once and had had his heart broken a time or two back then, but not since he'd come west after the late unpleasantness. Maybe he'd been lucky.

Pettigrew put the cork in the bottle. "Well, hell, I wish we could while away the afternoon here, but I reckon we'd best be gettin' on down to the courthouse."

"That police lieutenant'll sic his dogs on us, happen we don't show up on time," Wilburn said. He looked at the corked bottle in disappointment, too, then reached across the table and snagged it, tucking it under his coat. "For later," he said. He dropped some coins on the table to pay for the drinks and the bottle.

The four men got up and strolled out of the bar. As they entered the lobby, Longarm saw Ben Price and Jessamine Langley coming down the stairs. Price looked uncomfortable in a town suit, but Jessamine was lovely in a pink dress and hat. She looked more like she was going to a ball than an inquest.

Price and Jessamine joined the group of Longarm, Pettigrew, Schilling, and Wilburn. Maureen Mullaney came down to the lobby a few minutes later, along with several

91

other members of the Wild West Show troupe. Tom Beaumont was among them, and Longarm saw the glance he cast toward Price and Jessamine. It was dark and narrow-eyed, and Longarm didn't doubt for a second that Beaumont still felt a heap of resentment toward the head wrangler. That was something to bear in mind, Longarm told himself.

The large group walked together to the courthouse, which was only a few blocks away. The courtroom in which the inquests were held was crowded with witnesses, not to mention spectators. The coroner's jury was sworn in, and the rest of the afternoon was taken up by testimony in the two cases. Ben Price stubbornly insisted that he had seen some sort of flash just as the stampede started, and his testimony was enough to convince the jury not to make a ruling of accidental death concerning Alf Culpepper. The case was continued, pending further investigation by the authorities.

In the case of the still unidentified would-be payroll thief, the evidence was much more cut-and-dried. After the testimony of the witnesses, the foreman of the coroner's jury stood up and said, "We find that this gent died at the hands of Marshal Custis Long, who was acting justifiably and in self-defense. We recommend that no charges be filed against Marshal Long."

That was good enough for the coroner, who declared the case closed.

Lieutenant McClain, who had been sitting in the back of the courtroom, came up to Longarm afterwards and said, "You can go back to Denver now. I don't need you for my investigation into Culpepper's death."

Longarm inclined his head toward the members of the Wild West Show, who were filing out of the courtroom. "What about them? You going to hold them or let them go on to the next stop on their tour?"

McClain grimaced. "Unless I come up with some new evidence, I suppose I'll have to let them go. I can't hold them indefinitely just on suspicion."

Longarm was glad to hear that. Pettigrew had mentioned earlier that tonight's show would be the last one in Kansas City; tomorrow the troupe would be boarding a train that would take them to Denver.

Longarm intended to be on that train, too.

It was late afternoon when Longarm reached the hotel where he was staying. He hoped that Katherine Nash hadn't already come by there looking for him. She didn't know anything about the other mess involving Colonel Pettigrew's Wild West Show; Katherine's—and the Bureau of Indian Affair's—only interest was in Princess Little Feather

Longarm went to the desk and asked the clerk, "Has a lady been asking about me? Sort of refined-looking, mighty pretty with ash blonde hair?"

The man shook his head. "Not while I've been on duty, Marshal." He glanced at the little cubbyholes on the wall behind him where keys were kept. "And there's no note in your box."

"Much obliged." Longarm took his key and went upstairs.

The matchstick between the door and the jamb was right where he had left it the last time he went out, so he knew the place hadn't been disturbed. He went inside, tossed his hat on the bed, then took off his coat, vest, tie, and shirt so that he could wash up.

It seemed strange that less than twenty-four hours had passed since Katherine Nash had knocked on his door. A great deal had happened during that time: the stampede at the Wild West Show, the night of slap-and-tickle with Maureen Mullaney, someone getting into his hotel room for reasons still unknown, the attempted theft of the show's payroll and the resulting shoot-out, the fight at Cherokee Hank's, the creekside lovemaking with Maureen, and the inquests at the courthouse. Longarm gave a little shake of his head as he reached for a clean shirt. Events sure had kept him hopping, all right.

Knuckles rapped on the door.

93

Longarm had the shirt halfway on. He finished shrugging into it but left it unbuttoned. He hadn't taken off the cross-draw rig while he washed, so he reached across his body and snagged the Colt. Feeling better with the walnut grips of the gun smooth against his palm, he went to the door and called softly, "Who is it?" He was ready to dive either way if somebody started blasting through the door or the wall.

The feminine voice that answered made him feel a little foolish, but only a little. Being careful was a damned good habit for a lawman to get into.

"It's Katherine Nash."

Longarm twisted the key and stepped back. "It's open."

Katherine turned the knob and swung the door into the room. Longarm had lowered his Colt, but he still held it at his side. Katherine started to step into the room, then spotted the gun and stopped short. "Marshal Long?" she said.

Longarm could see by now that she was alone. He holstered the revolver and said, "Come on in, Miss Nash. Don't worry about the gun. Fella in my line of work is just naturally cautious."

"Yes, I suppose so," she said, her eyebrows arching a little. She came into the room and closed the door behind her.

Longarm became aware that, without the gun to focus on, Katherine's gaze had settled on his bare chest. He started buttoning up the shirt, and though he might have been mistaken, he could have sworn that he saw a flicker of disappointment in Katherine Nash's eyes.

"Well, Marshal," she said, "what did you find out about Princess Little Feather? Can we report to Chief Lame Bear that his long-lost daughter has finally been found?"

"I'm afraid not," Longarm replied. "Princess Little Feather ain't a Pawnee princess. Fact is, she's not any kind of Indian at all."

Now Katherine definitely looked disappointed. "You're sure about that?"

"Certain sure. She's really an Irish gal named Maureen Mullaney."

Katherine sighed. "It was just wishful thinking, I suppose, but I was hoping against hope that the chief would turn out to be right about her. I knew the chances of that were small, but still—"

"I reckon it would've been nice if it had worked out that way," Longarm agreed. "To tell the truth, though, I imagine that little Pawnee gal was either killed in the battle or carried off by one of the soldiers. If that was what happened, she probably wound up in a crib somewhere, working as a, uh, soiled dove."

"A prostitute, you mean. A whore."

Longarm shrugged. "Well, to be blunt about it, yeah."

Katherine sighed again and shook her head. "Such a shame. I was really hoping to do some good."

"I'm sure you do a lot of good," Longarm told her.

Her smile was wan. "It's a losing battle most of the time. There's only so much one person, or even one agency, can do, especially when there's so little funding available . . ."

Longarm wasn't going to argue politics with her. As far as he was concerned, that was like pounding sand down a rat hole. Instead he said, "If it would cheer you up any, ma'am, I'd sure admire to take you out to dinner this evening."

"Oh, no, I couldn't," Katherine quickly replied.

"Why not? You got to eat, and I do, too. And I hear tell there's a place down the street that serves mighty fine steaks."

"Well . . ." She wavered. "I suppose it wouldn't do any harm . . ."

" 'Course not. Let me get my coat and tie on."

Katherine stepped closer to him and rested a hand on his arm. "On behalf of the Bureau, let me thank you for your efforts, Marshal."

"It was my pleasure," Longarm assured her. Just like it was his pleasure to stand there with her only a foot or so away from him, her fingers warm on his flesh through the sleeve of his shirt, the sweet scent of wildflowers lingering about her. Whatever sort of perfume she was wearing, it was damned nice, he thought.

He saw the way her eyes went sort of heavy-lidded as she looked up at him. She was breathing faster now, her small breasts rising and falling quickly. Her hand was still resting on his arm.

Longarm thought about it for a moment, then gave a mental shrug. *What the hell.*

He leaned over and kissed her.

He had kissed female BIA agents before. Just like the others, Katherine Nash reacted as a woman, not a bureaucrat. She moved into his arms as they went around her. She was slender but still a warm, vital armful, Longarm found as his embrace tightened. She pressed her body to his, and her lips parted under his mouth. Their tongues met, probing and exploring.

Suddenly, Katherine pulled back, breaking the kiss. She put her hands on Longarm's chest, and while she didn't shove hard against him, she made it plain that she wanted to be let go. He obliged, never having been one to grab on to a woman if she didn't want to be grabbed.

"That . . . that was very unprofessional of you, Marshal," Katherine panted.

Longarm felt a brief flash of anger but reined it in. "What about you, ma'am?" he said coolly. "Seems to me it was just as much your idea as it was mine."

Katherine gasped. "That's not true! *You* kissed *me.*"

"Yes, ma'am," agreed Longarm. "But you wanted me to."

Katherine drew a deep breath. "I'm not going to have this argument with you, Marshal. I'm not going to dignify your comments with any sort of rebuttal."

That was because she'd have to lie in order to keep arguing, Longarm thought. She could call it anything she wanted, but they both knew the truth.

"I reckon you don't want to have dinner with me after all," he commented.

"On the contrary. I don't see why two *professionals* can't share a meal."

"Well, then . . . why don't I meet you down in the lobby in a couple of minutes?"

She nodded. "Very well. I'll be waiting for you."

When she was gone, Longarm shook his head and smiled. Miss Katherine Nash kept herself buttoned up pretty good, he thought. It must have spooked the hell out of her when she found herself in the arms of a man who was practically a stranger, kissing him for all she was worth and getting kissed the same way. Longarm couldn't help but wonder what it would be like for the fella who was lucky enough to be with her when she finally let herself go.

That fella wouldn't be him, he thought. After tonight's dinner, he would likely never see Katherine again. Come tomorrow, he'd be on the train heading back to Denver.

But he would have a fond memory of the moment that had just passed between them, and sometimes that was enough.

Sometimes it had to be.

97

Chapter 10

The steaks at the restaurant down the street were every bit as good as Longarm had heard they were, tender enough to cut with a fork and bursting with flavor. Add on a pile of potatoes and vegetables and dinner rolls so warm that steam rose from them when you tore them open, and you had one hell of a fine meal, he thought. Katherine seemed to enjoy the food, too, although being a female and on the dainty side at that, she didn't eat nearly as much as he did. Probably not even half as much.

Had he not been such a gentleman, when he was finished he would have liked to lean back, unfasten the top button on his trousers, and belch a couple of times. That would have been crude, though, so he suppressed the impulse. Had Katherine known what a sacrifice he was making, he was sure she would have thanked him for it.

As it was, she smiled, sipped from the glass of wine the waiter had brought to the table, and said, "There. Wasn't that enjoyable? A simple dinner shared by two colleagues, two fellow professionals."

"That's right," Longarm said, but he hadn't forgotten what else they had shared—that kiss up in his hotel room.

"What are you going to do now, Marshal?" Katherine asked. "I suppose you'll be going back to Denver as soon as possible."

Longarm nodded. "There's a train leaving in the morning. I figure to be on it."

"I've never been to Denver," she said, almost wistfully, and for a second Longarm thought she was hinting that she wanted to go with him. Then she went on, much more crisply, "Oh, well, I suppose I shall someday if my work ever happens to take me there."

Longarm was glad he hadn't issued an invitation. Katherine surely would have refused it.

For another moment, however, he considered asking her to accompany him to the Wild West Show tonight. He planned to attend the final performance so that he could see it all the way through, and also so that he would be on hand if any more trouble broke out. On reflection, he decided it might not be a good idea to take Katherine with him. If he did, Maureen was liable to see the two of them together, and then she'd probably get the wrong idea—or the right idea, depending on how you looked at it. And since Longarm was planning to enjoy Maureen's company during the train ride to Denver, he supposed it would be much better not to complicate matters.

That was the way of the world, he told himself. A fella couldn't have *everything*. Sometimes he had to pick and choose, and in this case, he chose Maureen.

As they left the restaurant, Longarm linked his arm with Katherine's arm and said, "I'll see you back to your hotel."

Deftly, she disengaged her arm. "I'm sure that's not necessary, Marshal."

"I insist. Ain't no telling what you'll run into in a big city like this, especially after dark."

"Kansas City is a civilized place," Katherine said. "I'm certain that a lady can walk its streets safely, no matter what the hour."

Longarm frowned. "I don't mind—"

"I do," Katherine cut in firmly. "Our business is over, Marshal, and pleasant though it was, so is our dinner. It's time for us to go our separate ways."

Longarm didn't much like that idea, but Katherine

wouldn't be convinced otherwise. He nodded and said, "All right, then, if that's what you want."

"It is," she said. She held out a gloved hand. "Good-bye, Marshal."

Longarm hesitated a second, then took her hand and shook it. "So long, Miss Nash. *Vaya con Dios.*"

Evidently she understood enough Spanish to be able to translate that phrase. She said, "You, too, Marshal Long."

Longarm thumbed his hat back on his head as he watched her walk away. There was no figuring some folks, and he supposed Katherine Nash was one of them.

Then, with a shake of his head, he turned toward the livery stable, intending to reclaim the horse he had rented earlier.

He had a Wild West Show to attend.

Longarm saw quite a few people standing in line at the ticket booth when he arrived at the fairgrounds arena. He swung down from the saddle and tied the reins to a hitch rack where several other mounts had already been tethered. Tonight he didn't feel much like standing in line and buying a ticket like everyone else, even though he was usually pretty much of an egalitarian sort, so he lit a cheroot and strolled around toward the back of the arena, thinking that surely he could find a rear entrance.

The sun had gone down while he was dining with Katherine Nash, and by now it was full night. The front of the arena, where the main entrance was located, was brightly lit, but around in back was less so. In fact, there was only one small, lonely lamp burning over a narrow door in the rear wall of the building. Longarm spotted it as he rounded the corner.

He spotted something else, too—movement in the thick shadows not far away. His teeth clenched on the cheroot and he took an instinctive step backward so that the corner would provide him with some cover if whoever was lurking back here started blazing away at him. His hand went to the butt of his gun.

100

The person in the shadows wasn't interested in bush-whacking him, however. People, rather, because there were two of them, he realized a moment later when he heard a woman's soft laugh, then a man's voice, rough with passion. Longarm couldn't make out the words the man spoke, but there was no mistaking the tone.

He dropped the cheroot in the dirt and quietly ground it out with the heel of his boot. He didn't want his presence given away by the smell of tobacco smoke drifting to the two people behind the arena. Longarm couldn't have said why he didn't just turn around and leave the lovers to their rendezvous. Maybe it was because there were warning bells faintly going off in the back of his head.

Easing closer to the corner, he leaned his shoulder against the brick wall and listened intently. Once again he heard the woman's laugh, then the man said, "I just don't understand you, honey. Why do you torture me this way?"

"I'm sorry, Tom," the woman replied, but Longarm didn't think her regret sounded completely genuine. "I'm just waiting for the right moment to tell Ben. You know that. You know how easily upset he is. I don't want him to cause any trouble for you."

Tom Beaumont snorted in contempt. "I'm not afraid of Price. Let him do his worst—"

"Hush, now," Jessamine Langley said. "Let's not talk about Ben. Just kiss me, Tom. Please, just kiss me . . ."

The silence that followed told Longarm that Beaumont was doing exactly what Jessamine had told him to do. Longarm listened anyway, his eyes narrowing in thought.

So the pretty trick rider was up to even more tricks, he mused. Jessamine was playing Tom Beaumont and Ben Price against each other, and from what Longarm had heard about the history of those three, she had evidently been up to her mischief for quite a while. Longarm was willing to bet that when Jessamine had been openly involved with Beaumont before, she had been carrying on behind his back with Price. Now the situation was just the opposite.

One thing was the same, though. Jessamine was getting lots of romantic attention from two men.

That was plumb interesting, Longarm decided. For one thing, it made even more plausible the theory that Beaumont had had something to do with the stampede the night before, and that Ben Price had been the real target.

Longarm heard some heavy breathing and the rustle of clothes. He wasn't sure just how much fooling around Jessamine and Beaumont could get up to back here in the shadows, but he had heard enough. He turned and walked silently toward the front of the building. Looked like he was going to stand in line after all.

That turned out not to be the case. Colonel Jasper Pettigrew was outside the arena, smiling and gladhanding and greeting the crowd in booming, jovial tones. The colonel spotted Longarm and waved him over.

"Howdy, Marshal," Pettigrew welcomed him. The colonel was wearing his buckskin jacket and big white Stetson again. "I was afraid you were goin' to miss the show, and this bein' our final performance in Kansas City."

"I would've had a chance to see it in Denver in a few days," Longarm said. "I'm heading back there tomorrow. I expect we'll be on the same train."

Pettigrew slapped him on the back. "Now, ain't that dandy! I'm glad to hear it, Marshal. You go on inside now and have yourself a fine ol'time!"

"I ain't bought a ticket yet," Longarm said, gesturing toward the booth.

"Oh, hell, don't worry about that!" Pettigrew waved him on up the ramp that led into the arena. "The show's on me tonight. Fact, I want you to sit in my private box. Come on, I'll show you where it is."

Pettigrew took the big lawman's arm and led him into the arena. Longarm went along without arguing, knowing that it wouldn't do any good against Pettigrew's bluster.

The colonel's private box was the best seat in the house, in the front of the grandstand midway around the arena.

102

Longarm would have the best possible view from here. He said, "I'm sure obliged to you, Colonel."

"Don't think a thing of it, son. You're the only one—I say, you're the only one who's believed me about that damned Cherokee Hank bein' to blame for all our troubles."

Longarm didn't say anything. He didn't point out that he hadn't actually come to that conclusion. It was just as likely in his mind, maybe even more likely, that Trenton was innocent of any wrongdoing where Pettigrew's show was concerned. Longarm might have a better idea of that if he was able to stick with the show on the trip back to Denver.

The big crowd was settling into the seats. Colonel Pettigrew went on his way, leaving Longarm alone in the private box. The box was open all the way around, but it had a railing with a gate in it to keep out anybody who wasn't supposed to be there. The seats here were nicer, too, actual chairs instead of backless benches, and with more room between the rows so that a fella could stretch out his legs a little. Longarm did so and fired up another cheroot, since he hadn't gotten to finish the one he'd started earlier. He shook out the lucifer and dropped it under his chair.

As he smoked, he thought about what he had discovered tonight about Jessamine and Beaumont. He was going to have to keep an eye on the wrangler, he decided.

The arena wasn't full, but at least three-fourths of the seats were occupied when the performance got under way. Longarm wondered if that was enough to be profitable for the colonel. Profitable or not, the troupe put on a fine show. Colonel Pettigrew welcomed the audience with the same sort of booming enthusiasm he had displayed outside. The grand entrance found dozens of men and women on horseback parading into the arena, the ones in the front rank carrying an assortment of colorful flags. When that was over, Jessamine Langley came out on a big white stallion to do her riding tricks. She was garbed in a scanty red and blue outfit with lots of spangles and feathers on it. The men in the audience seemed to enjoy the costume as much as they did the riding tricks, especially when Jessamine circled close to the grandstand so that they got a good view of her calves clad in silk stockings.

Jessamine was good, Longarm had to admit that. She could ride hanging from either side of the horse, like a Comanche. She rode backwards, then lifted herself and spun around so that she was facing forward again. Another horse was led into the arena, this time a black stallion, and she transferred from one to the other and back as they galloped side by side at top speed around the arena. Finally, she did the old Roman riding trick, standing up with her legs straddled, one foot on the saddle of each horse, as they galloped along in perfect tandem. Longarm watched the way her knees flexed, keeping her body almost perfectly still. That was the key to the trick. Longarm had seen a couple of Texas cowboys who could do it better, but Jessamine was almost as good.

She had the audience whooping and hollering and applauding as she left, then came back for a bow. Longarm banged his hands together like everybody else.

Jessamine was going to be a hard act to follow. That chore fell to Maureen, who came out in her Princess Little Feather getup as the show's musicians started beating on some drums to sound vaguely like Indian tom-toms. Longarm smiled. More than once, he'd heard the real thing pounding out a rhythm of death. This music was just a pale imitation of that.

The storekeepers and clerks and their families in the audience didn't know that, though. They enjoyed it. And Longarm had to admit that Maureen made a fetching picture in the tight buckskin dress and dark makeup and black wig. If he hadn't known it was her under all that, he might not have recognized her. As it was, though, he already knew her well enough to recognize some of the distinctive movements she made.

She started off making trick shots with a rifle, glorified target practice, really. She shot bottles off a stand, then plates that an assistant started spinning. After a while she put the rifle aside and changed to the six-guns that were holstered in a cartridge belt strapped around her trim hips. She did fast draws, fancy draws, flipped one of the guns from one hand to the other and back again in the border shift, bent over and shot between her legs, used a mirror to shoot over her shoulder at a target. All the while, Colonel Pettigrew was bellowing through a megaphone some maudlin, tragic story about how Princess Little Feather was the last true princess of the Pawnee tribe and how she had been orphaned when a flash flood had wiped out her village and left her to make her way in the hostile world of the white man . . . It was strictly dime-novel stuff, Longarm thought, which meant that Kurt Schilling, the Prussian bookkeeper, probably ate it up. Schilling might even have been responsible for some of the more melodramatic embellishments.

The crowd seemed to enjoy Maureen's part of the show every bit as much as Jessamine's. Longarm was glad to see that. The ovation Maureen received when she took her bows was just as loud, too. Longarm put two fingers in his mouth and let out a piercing whistle of admiration. Maureen wasn't too far away. She glanced up at him, met his eyes, and grinned. She gave him a wave as she turned and trotted toward the gate where the performers made their entrances and exits.

After Maureen's act, some of the show's wranglers rode wild, bucking broncs, the sort of thing that cowboys did in rodeos. Longarm had been down in Pecos, Texas, a year or so earlier when the first ever rodeo was staged, and they were catching on throughout the West, he'd heard.

The next act was a mock stagecoach robbery, after which a "posse" chased down the "outlaws" and shot it out with them in a thunderous fusillade of blank cartridges that turned the air blue with powder smoke. Again, Longarm had seen enough of the real thing to be aware of all the flaws and discrepancies and downright silliness of this staged villainy, but he looked on tolerantly.

Next, and last, on the agenda was the battle royal between the cavalry and the Indians. That would take some

105

time to set up, so Colonel Pettigrew advised the crowd to take advantage of the opportunity to purchase cotton candy and bags of peanuts and saltwater taffy from the fellas who would be circulating through the grandstand. Longarm wondered if the colonel got a cut of that money, too. It seemed pretty likely to him.

A thin haze of smoke still floated in the air from the shoot-out between the fake lawmen and desperadoes. A whiff of it reached Longarm's nose, and he sniffed, frowning as it struck him that something was different about the smoke. He had smelled enough burned powder in his time to be intimately familiar with its acrid tang. This wasn't the same, he realized. This smelled more like wood burning, mixed with something else, an odd, unfamiliar scent.

And it was getting stronger instead of fading away.

More smoke drifted past his face. He looked around, then looked down, stiffening as he peered underneath the grandstand and saw a flickering reddish glow. With a sudden surge of muscles, he came to his feet.

Something thudded into the back of the seat where he had just been sitting, and splinters stung the back of his left hand.

Ambush!

Longarm flung himself down in the aisle between the rows of seats in the private box. They wouldn't be much shelter from the bushwhacker's bullets, but they were better than nothing. He grabbed his Colt and looked around, searching urgently for the location of the rifleman who had come so close to ventilating him. And while having a would-be killer somewhere in the arena gunning for him was bad enough, it wasn't his only problem, he realized grimly.

Unless he was wrong, the whole damned place was on fire.

Chapter 11

Longarm wasn't the only one to have smelled the smoke and seen the flames. Somewhere in the grandstand, someone shouted, "Fire!" Closer to the colonel's private box, some of the spectators had seen the bushwhacker's bullet strike Longarm's chair, and they had also seen the big lawman dive for cover and yank out his gun. A couple of women screamed in fear, and men yelled angrily.

Panic spread like a prairie fire. People surged to their feet, yelling and screaming and crying. They grabbed their children and headed pell-mell for the exits, trampling anybody who got in their way. In practically the blink of an eye, the entire arena was filled with chaos.

That worked in his favor, Longarm realized as he came up in a crouch, the Colt still gripped tightly in his fist. With hundreds of people running around like they were, it would be difficult if not impossible for the bushwhacker to pick him out of the fear-crazed crowd.

The air was filling with smoke now, and actual flames licked up through the openings between the rows of benches in the grandstand not far from Pettigrew's box. Most of the spectators had already managed to get away from that area, Longarm saw. Then his gaze fell on a little boy, maybe four years old, who was just sitting there three or four rows away, his face contorted from crying. He was obviously too scared to move, and his family had run off and left him, perhaps accidentally or maybe they were just too worried about their own hides to care. Either way, Longarm knew he couldn't just leave the kid sitting there.

Of course, by venturing out into that area where it was clearer, he might be exposing himself to the hidden rifleman's shots once again.

Didn't matter, Longarm decided. The way the blaze was spreading, that section of the grandstand might collapse in a few minutes. If it did, the terrified youngster would be lost for sure.

Longarm straightened, put his free hand on the railing around the private box, and vaulted over it, not taking the time to open the gate. As he landed on the other side, a slug smacked off the railing a couple of feet from his hand.

Blast it! thought Longarm. The bushwhacker was still out there somewhere. Longarm had hoped that the gunman would have fled like nearly everybody else.

With long strides, Longarm bounded up the grandstand toward the abandoned child, leaping from bench to bench. He didn't know if any more bullets came fanging after him or not. The tumult in the arena was too loud to hear any shots, and he didn't look behind him to see if slugs were kicking up splinters from the grandstand. He kept his attention focused on the kid.

The little boy saw him coming and looked even more scared, but he still didn't budge. Longarm reached the kid, bent over, and scooped him up. As he did so, a gout of flame burst through the grandstand to his left, and another flared out above him. Longarm wheeled around and started back down the rows of benches. If he couldn't get out one way, he would go another.

The smoke in the air was so thick now that it was difficult to see. Again, Longarm realized that could work in his favor. With all that smoke, the bushwhacker wouldn't be able to line sights on him. Of course, there was also the possibility that he and the kid would choke to death, Longarm thought. The kid was already coughing, and the acrid smoke stung the back of Longarm's throat.

He reached the edge of the grandstand, flames licking at his heels. Longarm bounded to the top of the railing and leaped out into space, cradling the child against him as he did so. The drop to the floor of the arena was about eight feet, he remembered. He landed on his feet and went down into a roll to lessen the impact, keeping his body turned so that he bore the brunt of it and protected the little boy.

Longarm's hat had gone flying, but he managed to hang on to his gun. He came to his feet and stumbled toward the spot where he thought the big gate was located, though with the air so clogged with smoke it was hard to be sure of anything. If he could reach the gate, he thought he could find his way through the dressing room area and the corrals and make it out of the building that way.

Suddenly, a horse loomed up out of the smoke, galloping straight at Longarm and the kid. The horse was as crazed by fear as anyone else in the arena. Longarm flung himself aside, holding tightly to the child, and let the animal thunder on past.

Longarm staggered on, starting to cough now. He glanced over his shoulder, saw that an entire section of the grandstand was fully ablaze. If the fire reached the roof of the building, things would get really bad.

Another horse came out of the smoke, but this one had a rider. "Custis!" Maureen Mullaney shouted. "Custis, where are you?"

"Here!" Longarm bellowed. Maureen turned the horse, spotted him, and rode toward him. When she reached him, she reined in, and he handed the little boy up to her. "Gimme that stirrup!"

Maureen took her foot out of the stirrup, and Longarm used it to swing up onto the horse's back behind the saddle. He put his arms around her waist and said into her ear, "Get us out of here!"

She kicked the horse into a run. The open gate became visible through the smoke in front of them. The horse galloped through it and along the wide, hard-packed dirt runway that led to the corrals. The smoke wasn't as bad here, and Longarm gratefully drew in several lungfuls of the clearer air.

The corral gates were all open, and so were the big doors through which horses and wagons could enter and leave the arena building. Maureen guided her mount through one of the doors and into the open night air. Longarm saw people and animals everywhere, and all of them were still scared. He heard a loud, clamorous clanging and recognized it as the bells on fire trucks. The horse-drawn steam pumpers of the Kansas City fire department had arrived on the scene, although Longarm wasn't sure how much good they were going to be able to do. The blaze was too well-established by now.

Maureen pulled the horse to a stop a good distance away from the burning building. Longarm slid down to the ground and reached up for the little boy. "I'll take him now," he told Maureen.

She lowered the still-sobbing child into Longarm's hands. "Who is he?"

"Damned if I know," replied Longarm. "His folks must've run off and left him, but I knew I couldn't."

Maureen dismounted. She was still wearing the buckskin dress and the makeup, but she had lost the black wig somewhere in the confusion. Her thick red hair had fallen loose around her shoulders.

"How'd you know to come looking for me?" Longarm asked her.

"I was helping to get some of the horses out when I saw you jump off the railing around the grandstand. When we got to the corrals, I grabbed the first horse I could find with a saddle on it and came back for you."

"I'm much obliged," Longarm told her with a tired smile, "and I reckon this little tyke would be, too, if he wasn't too scared to think about it right now."

"You're going to have to find his family," Maureen pointed out.

"Yeah, I reckon. Or at least somebody'll have to find them."

Longarm had already spotted Lieutenant McClain coming toward them, followed as usual by several uniformed officers. McClain was red-faced and blustering, but he was surprised into momentary speechlessness when Longarm handed him the little boy and said, "Here you go, Lieutenant. Got a stray for you."

McClain looked down at the kid, who burst into a fresh round of sobs. Grating a curse, McClain turned and thrust the boy into the hands of one of the officers. "Here, Leland. Find out who this brat belongs to."

When McClain turned back to him, Longarm said, "I think you scared the kid even worse than the fire, Lieutenant."

McClain ignored the comment and demanded harshly, "Why do I find you around every time there's trouble, Long?"

"Just lucky, I reckon," Longarm said.

McClain glowered. He jerked a thumb over his shoulder at the burning building. "What happened here?"

The fire wagons were pouring streams of water into the arena. Longarm watched them for a second, then said, "Looks pretty obvious, Lieutenant. The arena caught on fire."

"Or somebody set it on fire," snapped McClain.

Longarm shrugged. "Could be."

He didn't say anything about the shots that an unknown rifleman had taken at him. It was entirely possible that there was no connection between the bushwhack attempt and the conflagration. Longarm was certain of only one thing:

The fire *might* have been accidental, but the attempt on his life was deliberate. He intended to find that bushwhacker himself.

Longarm maintained his facade of ignorance as McClain badgered him for several more minutes. Finally, the policeman gave up in disgust and turned to Maureen. "What

111

about you?" he asked. "Did you see anything that would explain what happened?"

"Princess Little Feather no see-um anything, white man," Maureen answered.

The lieutenant growled an obscenity. "You're not an Indian princess!" he exclaimed. "Not with that red hair!"

"I still didn't see anything," Maureen replied calmly. "In fact, I was already in my dressing room when I heard all the commotion. I came back out to see what was going on, and I realized the building was on fire."

"What were you doing with Long here?"

"I saw him and rode back inside to help him get out."

"Why would you do that?" McClain demanded.

"Because he's my friend," Maureen said, and she smiled at Longarm.

McClain grumbled, threw up his hands, and walked off to question the other bystanders. There were hundreds of them, including the members of the Wild West Show and many of the people who had been in the audience, so he had his work cut out for him.

"I'm afraid I wasn't quite truthful with the lieutenant," Maureen said to Longarm when McClain was gone.

"How's that?" asked Longarm.

"The real reason I went back in there to save you is because you're better in bed than any man I've ever known."

Longarm let out a laugh. "Glad I'm good for *something*," he said dryly.

"And I think you're a pretty nice man, too," Maureen added.

"Well, I appreciate what you did, riding back in there like that. Could've got yourself killed, though."

"It was a chance I was willing to take," Maureen said with a smile.

Longarm was giving serious thought to kissing her, when Colonel Pettigrew bustled up, wringing his hands and saying, "Dadgum it all! This is goin' to ruin us!"

112

"Will it really, Colonel?" Longarm asked. "How much did you lose?"

"I don't rightly know yet, but it's bound to be bad."

Maureen said, "I think we got most of the horses out. We shouldn't lose more than one or two of them. I saw Ben driving the stagecoach out, too, so it should be safe."

"What about the Conestoga?" Pettigrew asked.

Maureen shook her head. "I didn't see it, so it may be lost. And I'm sure if the fire spread to the dressing rooms, we'll lose some of the costumes, too."

"Tarnation!" exclaimed Pettigrew. "Ain't there no end to the deviltry that bastard'll pull to ruin me?"

"You're talking about Cherokee Hank?" Longarm asked. "Who else?"

Longarm didn't think even Trenton would burn down a building and risk the lives of hundreds of people in order to damage a business rival. Blinded by his hatred of the man, though, it was doubtful that Colonel Pettigrew would be able to see things that way.

"Fires break out on their own sometimes," Longarm pointed out.

Stubbornly, Pettigrew shook his head. "After the way everything else has gone wrong for us the past few weeks, I don't believe in accidents no more." He smacked his right fist into his left palm. "No, sir, this is Trenton's doin'! I feel it in my bones."

Longarm wasn't going to waste his time arguing with the colonel's bones. He turned to Maureen and said, "There's nothing else we can do here. Why don't I see that you get back to the hotel all right?"

"That sounds good to me," Maureen agreed. She reached for the reins of the mount she had ridden back into the blazing arena.

"Why don't you let the wranglers handle that horse?" Longarm suggested. "I've got one that I rented from a livery stable, if it's still around front where I left it before the show started."

The horse was still there, though it was definitely

spooked by the noise and the smell of smoke and everything else that had happened. Longarm considered himself lucky that the animal hadn't snapped its reins and run off. He swung up into the saddle and then helped Maureen up in front of him.

Their positions were reversed now, since he'd ridden behind her on the mad dash out of the burning building. As they rode back through Kansas City toward The Cattlemen's Hotel, Longarm found that he liked this setup much better. He held the reins in his right hand and slipped his left arm around Maureen's waist. Her firm rump was snuggled up against his groin, and every step the horse took made the tantalizing contact even more arousing. Maureen must have felt his shaft hardening against her, because she laughed and said, "I didn't realize I was sitting on the saddle horn."

Longarm moved his free hand up her body and cupped her left breast through the buckskin dress. He had come close to death more than once tonight. Touching Maureen like this was a powerful reminder that he was still alive despite the best efforts of whoever wanted him dead. And that was a mighty important thing to remember.

He dug his boot heels into the horse's flanks and clucked to it, urging it on toward the hotel at a faster gait.

"Are you in a hurry, Marshal?" Maureen asked in mock innocence.

"You'll see when we get there," Longarm said. "More than once."

He kept his promise. He made love to Maureen until both of them fell into a sated, exhausted slumber. The deep, dreamless sleep was just what Longarm needed.

He wasn't sleeping so soundly, however, that his internal alarm failed to wake him in time to catch the Denver train. After a moment of stretching, he sat up and reached over to rest a hand on the smooth, creamy, bare shoulder of Maureen Mullaney.

"Time to get up," Longarm said, giving her a little shake. "We've both got a train to catch."

Maureen let out a groan as she began to stir. She was lying with her back to Longarm. With a sensuous movement, she slid over in the bed and snuggled her backside against him. Longarm threw back the sheet and gave the enticing rump a swat.

"No time for that," he said.

Maureen rolled over, the red hair tumbling in disarray around her pouting face. "Don' wanna get up," she mumbled. She reached out, fumbling in Longarm's lap until her hand closed around his half-erect shaft. She bent over and said, "Want some of this," just before her lips closed around the head of his manhood.

Longarm's watch was still in the pocket of the vest he had hastily taken off the night before, so he wasn't sure what time it was. A glance at the light coming in the window told him that it was still fairly early. He sighed as he finished stiffening into a full erection. Maureen opened her mouth wider and swallowed more of it.

Some people needed a cup of coffee before they were woke up good in the morning, he thought. He supposed Maureen just needed a different sort of eye-opener.

A few minutes later, he gave it to her, his hips lifting involuntarily off the bed as he emptied himself into her greedily sucking mouth.

Ten minutes after that, they came downstairs fully dressed. Longarm wasn't all the way to what he considered bright-eyed and bushy-tailed—he would need a round of bacon or ham and flapjacks and hash browns and fried eggs, washed down with several cups of good strong Arbuckle's for that—but at least he was making progress toward feeling human again.

Maureen, on the other hand, looked wide awake and fresh as a daisy. She wore most of a bottle-green traveling outfit, having left only the hat up in her room. Arm in arm, she and Longarm entered the hotel dining room, and the lawman heard someone call his name.

He spotted Colonel Pettigrew, Asa Wilburn, and Kurt Schilling sitting together at one of the tables. Ben Price and

Jessamine Langley were at another table, and several other members of the Wild West Show, including Tom Beaumont, were scattered around the room having breakfast. Longarm and Maureen went over to join the colonel and his companions.

Pettigrew seemed to be considerably more cheerful this morning than he had been the night before. "Howdy," he greeted Longarm and Maureen. "You two have a good night?"

Maureen had the good grace to blush slightly. "I'm sure I don't know what you mean, Colonel," she said. "Marshal Long just came over to have breakfast with me."

"Uh-huh," Pettigrew said. He looked at Longarm. "That lieutenant fella from the police department came by a while ago. Said as far as they could determine, the fire started because somebody dropped a match down under the grandstand and caught some straw on fire that had blown under there."

Longarm frowned. He remembered dropping a lucifer, but he was certain he had shaken it out first. Besides, the blaze had started quite a while after that.

Still, the flames had first appeared right there in the area where he had been sitting. He felt a twinge of worry. He didn't like to think that he might have been responsible for all that damage, not to mention the danger to human life . . .

"Did McClain say if anybody was hurt bad?" Longarm asked.

"According to the lieutenant, no one was mortally injured," Schilling said. "There were some burns and some broken bones in the exodus of the spectators, but other than that everyone was exceedingly fortunate."

"And damned lucky, too," Wilburn put in. "Too bad about the horses, though."

"How many did the show lose?" Longarm asked.

"Three horses," Pettigrew said. "Could'a been a lot worse, I suppose. And the Conestoga wagon we use in the entrance parade, it burned up, too."

"You can replace three horses and a wagon," Longarm

116

said. "There's a wagon yard not far from here, in fact."

Pettigrew nodded. "I already been asking around about it. We're supposed to have a Conestoga delivered to the depot in time to load it on a flatcar before we pull out for Denver."

"The fire's not going to stop you from continuing with the tour, then?"

Pettigrew's fist thumped on the table. "Damn right it ain't! Hank's goin' to be mighty disappointed when he hears that we're still goin' to beat him to Denver."

"And all we had to do was agree to put off gettin' paid for a couple of weeks," drawled Wilburn.

"I told you, Asa, everybody'll get a bonus once we make back what we lost," Pettigrew promised. "You'll see. If we just stick together, everything will be all right."

There was a faint note of desperation in the colonel's voice, Longarm thought. He was still doubtful that Cherokee Hank Trenton had had anything to do with the fire, but even if the disaster was completely accidental, it might yet wind up benefitting Trenton's show. Everything that went wrong for Pettigrew, big or little, pushed the colonel's operation that much closer to the edge.

Pettigrew turned to Longarm. "How about you, Marshal? I recollect you sayin' something about goin' back to Denver yourself. Are you leavin' on the train this mornin'?"

Longarm nodded. "That's right. So I reckon I'll be traveling with you folks all the way there."

"It's good to know there will be a lawman along," Schilling said. "Although, once we are away from Kansas City, perhaps our luck will change."

"We can hope so," Longarm said.

But considering everything that had happened, he sort of doubted it. For one thing, somewhere out there, there was still some son-of-a-bitch bushwhacker who wanted him dead . . .

Chapter 12

Longarm stood on the observation platform at the rear of one of the passenger cars and smoked a cheroot as the train arrowed across the rolling plains. Several hours earlier, the big Baldwin locomotive with its eight-sided smokestack had pulled out of the depot in Kansas City, drawing behind it the long array of passenger cars, freight cars, and flatcars. Across the high trestle over the Missouri River, then through the smaller settlement on the western bank of the Big Muddy, then into the grasslands that stretched all the way to the Rockies, nearly seven hundred miles away. Once this vast prairie had been known as the Great American Desert. It was hard to understand how anybody could have ever regarded it as a desert, thought Longarm. Whoever had stuck that name on it likely had never seen it like this, with the grass thick and lush and still green from the spring rains, dotted with wildflowers that were bright little explosions of color. Longarm took a deep drag on the cheroot and blew the smoke out.

He would feel pretty good about things, he decided, if not for the fact that somebody had tried to kill him the night before.

He had come out here to think, something that was difficult to do while sitting on a hard bench seat in a smoky, rough-riding passenger car. The fresh air had done a good job of blowing the cobwebs out of his brain.

Whoever the bushwhacker was, he almost had to be connected to the Wild West Show, Longarm reasoned. The two other jobs he'd carried out in Kansas City—delivering that addle-pated soldier boy to the guards from Leavenworth, then checking on "Princess Little Feather" for the BIA— had been concluded with no complications. Neither of them should have led to an attempt on his life.

But somebody else in the Wild West Show, somebody with something to hide, could have panicked when a federal lawman came poking around. The situation got even worse when Alf Culpepper was killed in that stampede and Longarm's curiosity was piqued. He'd made himself a presence around the hotel and the arena, and the bushwhacker had decided that he had to get rid of the big star-packer.

Longarm's eyes narrowed as the wind blew smoke from the cheroot back into them. He blinked and turned slightly, so that the smoke was carried away by the rush of the train's passage across the prairie. His teeth clamped on the cheroot.

Of course, it was always possible that he'd been recognized by somebody who had an old grudge against him, he told himself. After years of carrying a badge, he had plenty of enemies. Hell, he couldn't kill *every* bad man who crossed paths with him. A lot of them had gone to prison, and some of them had done their time and gotten out. Of the ones he'd been forced to ventilate fatally, many of them had relatives who likely hadn't forgotten Longarm's role in those deaths. Surely, out of all the people in Kansas City, there was more than one who wouldn't have minded blowing a hole in his hide.

Still, Longarm didn't believe overmuch in coincidence. Until it was proven otherwise, he was going with the theory that the attempt on his life was connected with his poking around Colonel Pettigrew's operation.

The door into the car opened, and Longarm turned his head to see Asa Wilburn stepping out onto the platform.

119

The lanky frontiersman wore a buckskin shirt and whipcord trousers tucked into high black boots. His broad-brimmed black hat was pushed back on his graying hair. The clothes didn't look like a costume on him, and for good reason: they, like him, were the genuine article.

Wilburn closed the door behind him and took out a pipe. Struggling a little in the wind, he packed tobacco in it and got it burning. Then he pointed to a wide, shallow depression in the earth a hundred yards or so south of the railroad tracks and said, "See that buffalo waller yonder? I stood off 'bout forty Kiowas one day whilst layin' in there."

"That a fact?" said Longarm.

A grin spread across Wilburn's leathery face. "Well, not really. There was only twenty of 'em, I reckon. But considerin' how many years ago that's been, I'd say the number just doublin' ain't too bad."

Longarm laughed. "When was that?"

"Lemme see . . .'54, I think. Maybe '55. It was before the war, I know that. But settlers had already started comin' in, so it wasn't long after that I headed on west."

Longarm inclined his head toward the railroad car. "How'd you come to hook up with this bunch?"

"Man can't make a livin' shootin' buffalo no more. All the herds are gone, 'cept for a few down in the Texas Panhandle. And those herds are so small it ain't even worthwhile to go after 'em no more." Wilburn shook his head. "Funny how much things can change in less'n twenty years. Ain't much frontier left no more."

Longarm wouldn't go so far as to say that. He'd been in some pretty desolate spots during his career, places where civilization still hadn't reached and maybe never would. But he didn't argue with Wilburn. Compared to what the West had been like when Wilburn was a youngster, it *had* changed a lot.

"Anyway," Wilburn went on after a moment, "I ran into the colonel in St. Louis, when he was first puttin' his show together last year. He asked me to go east with him, and I did. Figured it was time I started puttin' back a little money for my old age." He snorted. "Didn't realize how damned little it was goin' to be."

"Pettigrew's having a hard time keeping the show going, ain't he?"

Wilburn shrugged. "From what I hear tell, ol' Bill Cody's got hisself a pretty good show. I like the colonel, I reckon, but Cody's more of a showman, always has been. There might be room for a few more outfits like us and Cherokee Hank's, but not for all of 'em. Somebody'll go under, that's for damn sure."

Longarm nodded slowly. He agreed with Wilburn's assessment of the situation. Since they were alone on the platform, he asked bluntly, "Do you think Trenton's behind all the trouble Pettigrew's been having?"

"Naw, not really," Wilburn replied, surprising Longarm a little. "The colonel's one of them fellers who're just natural-born unlucky. But Hank's sharp enough to take advantage of that, right enough."

Longarm suspected Wilburn was right. That still left the unanswered question of who had tried to kill him.

He moved on to a different but maybe related topic. "How well do you know Ben Price?"

"The wrangler?" Wilburn shrugged again. "Pretty well, I guess. I don't spend a lot of time with those cowboys, maybe play a game of cards with 'em every now and then."

"Then you don't know Tom Beaumont all that well, either."

"Nope, I reckon not." Wilburn looked intently at Longarm and went on, "But I know those two boys don't like each other. And I know why."

"Jessamine Langley," Longarm said flatly.

Wilburn puffed on his pipe and nodded. "That little gal gets a pure-dee joy out of drivin' those boys crazy. Hell, she even tried to cozy up to me once, and I'm nigh old enough to be her grandpappy!"

That came as a surprise to Longarm. "Jessamine's not just playing Price and Beaumont against each other?"

"Well, there's some of that goin' on, all right. But from what I've seen, that gal's just plain hot-blooded. If every male in sight ain't pantin' after her, she ain't happy."

Longarm frowned and wondered if he ought to be offended that Jessamine hadn't made a play for him yet, if that was the case. Maybe she just hadn't gotten around to him, he consoled himself.

Wilburn was still watching him shrewdly. "You're wonderin' if maybe Beaumont started that stampede thinkin' that Ben Price was the one who'd get trampled, not Culpepper."

"It could have happened that way," Longarm said. It was the theory he'd been coming back to again and again, almost from the first.

Wilburn nodded. "Sure, I suppose it could've. Hadn't ever thought of it myself until just now."

"Keep it under your hat," Longarm requested. "If somebody like Beaumont really is making trouble, I don't want to spook him just yet."

"Give him enough rope to hang himself, eh? Sure, I'll keep quiet, Marshal. Hell, I'm just a broke-down old buffalo hunter. I ain't no sleuth."

Longarm didn't care much for detective work, either, but sometimes his job forced him into it. And sometimes, he supposed, he was just too damned curious for his own good.

The door of the car opened again, and Kurt Schilling joined Longarm and Wilburn on the platform. The bookkeeper was wearing a derby, and he put a hand on it to keep the wind from blowing it off. With his other hand, he thumped himself on the chest as he smiled at Longarm and Wilburn.

"Ah, fresh air!" Schilling said. "And the fresh, unspoiled vistas of your wonderful American landscape. This is why I came to your country."

"Wait'll you see the Rockies or the Tetons," advised Wilburn. "They're a heap prettier than this prairie."

"I am looking forward to that." Schilling took a small

metal case from his pocket and opened it, revealing several thin, dark brown cigarettes. He put one in his mouth and lit it with a kitchen match he also took from the case.

"What sort of ready-mades are those?" Longarm asked, nodding toward the cigarette.

"Egyptian," Schilling replied. "Would you like to try one?"

Longarm shook his head. "No, thanks. I'll stick with these three-for-a-nickel stogies of mine. I ain't cultured enough to appreciate anything fancier."

"On the contrary, Marshal, I think you are a much more cultured man than you let on."

"Well, I appreciate the sentiment," Longarm said with a grin, "but don't tell nobody. I got a reputation to uphold."

Schilling chuckled, and the three men smoked companionably for a while. Longarm didn't do any more theorizing about the events of the past few days, as he had done with Asa Wilburn. He wasn't sure he trusted Schilling quite enough for that.

By evening, the train had made stops in Topeka, Junction City, Abilene, and Salina. Longarm had stretched his legs on the depot platform at Abilene and seen a friendly reunion between Asa Wilburn and a massive man with a bushy gray beard. Wilburn called him Nestor, and they spent several minutes pounding each other on the back and turning the air blue with cheerful profanity. Nestor wore a deputy's badge, Longarm noticed, but he decided not to introduce himself to the man as a fellow star-packer.

"Old partner of yours?" Longarm asked Wilburn idly when the train was rolling west again.

Wilburn nodded. "Damn right. Been on many a hunt with him. Heard he went through some rough times when the herds moved south, so I was right glad to see that he's straightened hisself out."

The train was running a race with dusk now, staying just ahead of it for the time being. Night would win eventually, of course. Longarm wandered up toward the club car. It had been a long time since he'd eaten the stale sandwich and the apple he'd bought for lunch from a boy who went through the passenger cars selling them.

Maureen was sitting on a bench beside one of the windows in the club car. She smiled when Longarm came in. "Custis, you've been ignoring me all day," she accused. "Sit down here with me and have a drink."

"Don't mind if I do," Longarm said with an answering grin. He looked around and saw that the troupe had practically taken over the car. Colonel Pettigrew was seated at a large round table surrounded by members of the Wild West Show, Kurt Schilling, Ben Price, and Jessamine Langley among them. Longarm didn't see Tom Beaumont.

The bar stocked Maryland rye, a fact for which Longarm thanked the Good Lord and the Union Pacific railroad. He sipped from a glass of it as he sat with Maureen and watched night gradually overtake the train and spread its dark blanket over the prairie.

"Well, nothing else bad has happened since we left Kansas City," Maureen said. "It looks like Kurt was right. Our luck has changed."

Longarm took another sip of the whiskey. "I hope you're right," he said. "We ain't in Denver yet, though."

"Don't be so pessimistic."

"Comes with the territory," he said with a shrug. "Being a lawman, I reckon I just naturally see more bad than good."

She leaned closer to him and said quietly, "Later tonight, I'll show you something that's very good."

Longarm chuckled. Asa Wilburn had said that Jessamine was a hot-blooded sort, but as far as Longarm could tell, she didn't have anything on Maureen in that respect. Maureen, though, seemed to be content to focus all her sensual energy on one lucky gent at a time.

The only food available in the club car were more of the roast beef sandwiches like the one Longarm had eaten earlier in the day. The Maryland rye made the sandwich he ate now go down a little easier. Maureen settled for an apple. The train would stop at Hays early the next morning, and there was a Harvey House there, Longarm recalled. The passengers would be able to get a good breakfast, anyway.

Maureen yawned. "I'm tired," she said, lowering one eyelid in a wink directed at Longarm. "I think I'll go to bed."

The ladies in the troupe had berths in a sleeper, while the men were making do with sitting up in the club car or trying to snatch a few winks on the hard bench seats in the regular passenger cars. Discreetly, Maureen told Longarm which of the berths was hers.

"I'll expect to see you in half an hour," she murmured to him. "Don't keep me waiting. I'd hate to have to start without you."

Longarm reflected that that might not be such a bad thing to see, but wisely, he kept the thought to himself. Like every other man in the club car, he watched Maureen sashay out. That included Ben Price, Longarm noted. He saw that Jessamine had a slight frown on her pretty face. She must not like the fact that one of her beaus had dared to even look in the direction of another beautiful woman, he concluded.

After a few minutes, Jessamine said something to Price that made him look surprised and a little angry. She was probably laying down the law to him, Longarm thought. And Price wasn't taking it too well, either. He glared back at Jessamine and said something sharp. She stood up, snapped back at him, and then marched out of the club car.

Considering what Longarm knew about her and Tom Beaumont, Jessamine had a lot of nerve fussing at Price for looking at Maureen Mullaney. But that was the way of it with women; their actions didn't have to make sense all the time. Hell, nobody's did, male or female, Longarm told himself. He was just glad that he wasn't Ben Price right about now. He'd be licking the wounds from that sharp tongue of Jessamine's if he was.

A few minutes later, Longarm finished his drink and stood up. Colonel Pettigrew tried to call him over to join the roistering around the big table, but Longarm shook his head. "I'm a mite fired," he said with a casual wave. "Good night, gents."

Several of the men, including Kurt Schilling and Asa Wilburn, called good night to him. Longarm stepped out of the club car.

Habit made him cautious. Moving from light into darkness made a man vulnerable to all sorts of things, few if any of them good. But no gun blazed from the shadows, no club or fist or knife descended from the night, and so Longarm went on into the sleeping car without any trouble.

He made his way down the center aisle, which was dimly lit by a small lantern hanging at each end of the car. The berths had all been made up for the night. The dark curtains were pulled firmly across the openings. Maureen had told him that she was in the fourth lower berth on the left. As Longarm strolled toward it, he told himself that they would have to be pretty quiet with their romping tonight, otherwise whoever was in the upper berth would get a hell of an earful.

That was all right, he decided. Sometimes it was best to take things slow and easy and quiet.

A hand came out from behind the curtains on one of the upper berths on the right.

Longarm stopped short, instinct taking over and making his hand start toward the Colt holstered in the crossdraw rig on his left hip. He never completed the draw, because the hand protruding into the corridor wasn't holding any sort of weapon. The long, slender fingers were unmistakably feminine, as was the voice that whispered throatily, "Marshal Long?"

"Miss Langley?" Longarm said. "Is that you?"

The curtains were parted just enough for a blue eye to peer out at him. "Marshal Long," Jessamine said. "Thank God it's you. I was afraid that awful Ben Price had come back here to bother me again."

Longarm frowned. "Pardon me, ma'am, but I thought you and Price were sweethearts." He didn't let on that he'd seen the argument in the club car a short while earlier.

126

The curtains opened a little more. "I used to think Ben was sweet," Jessamine said, still whispering. "But he's gotten so . . . so possessive. He acts like he owns me!"

Longarm would have said it was the other way around, but he had more sense than to voice that opinion. Especially considering that the curtains over Jessamine's berth were parting more and more. In the dim light, Longarm saw quite a bit of pale, smooth flesh.

Jessamine was wearing some sort of light blue frippery, but it didn't amount to much, and it didn't cover much, either. She swung her legs out of the berth, and they were bare up to the knees. Pretty knees they were, too, Longarm noted, curved and dimpled just right.

Pushing the curtains back even more, Jessamine sat on the edge of her bunk and leaned out toward Longarm, giving him a good view down into the valley between her mostly exposed breasts. He saw her nipples poking out against the thin fabric.

"I'm frightened of Ben," she whispered. "You have to promise me, Marshal, that you'll protect me. It's your duty as a lawman, isn't it?"

"Reckon I'm supposed to look out for all law-abiding citizens, ma'am," Longarm said. It was all he could do not to laugh at Jessamine's heavy-handed play for his attentions. He didn't intend to accept the invitation she was throwing his way, but in the meantime, he was enjoying the free show. He figured he ought to feel guilty, but somehow he didn't.

"Thank you, Marshal. Thank you so much." Jessamine slid all the way out of her berth, the gauzy garment she wore swirling around her legs as she did so. She moved closer to Longarm and said, "I'd like to show you how much I appreciate your gallantry."

The corridor was deserted except for Longarm and Jessamine. The curtains were still closed over Maureen's berth. He could kiss this brazen little hussy and nobody would know. On the other hand, if he turned her down, she

127

was liable to get offended and raise a stink. The best thing to do was keep things quiet, he decided, and the best way to do that was to kiss Jessamine Langley just like she wanted.

He put his hands on her waist and she wound her arms around his neck. Longarm would have leaned over to kiss her, but she was a tall girl and when she came up on her toes he didn't have to reach very far to find her lips. Her body molded to his.

Well, Jessamine might have taken a while to get around to him, thought Longarm, but she was making up for lost time now. She kissed like a house afire, and despite Longarm's best intentions, he felt his shaft growing hard. Jessamine felt it, too, prodding against her belly. She worked her hips back and forth, caressing him with her body.

Longarm knew better than to get distracted. It happened anyway, as he was so caught up in the sensuousness of Jessamine's kiss that he didn't hear the curtain being pulled back quietly elsewhere in the sleeping car. He didn't even know that anyone else was around until a voice said stridently, "Let go of him, you whore!"

Then somebody grabbed Jessamine, jerked her out of his arms, and spun her around. A perfectly thrown right cross flashed through the air, and a fist smacked against Jessamine's jaw, throwing her back through the curtains of the berth behind her.

Oh, hell, thought Longarm. *Maureen.*

And all those old stories about redheads and Irish tempers . . . as he saw her green eyes flash fire, he knew they were all true.

128

Chapter 13

A startled yell came from the lower berth where Jessamine had gone sprawling. Longarm would have been surprised, too, if he'd been sleeping and some strange woman had fallen on him.

Jessamine came bolting back out of the berth, her face flushed with anger. She lunged at Maureen, shrieking, "You bitch!" She clawed at Maureen's eyes with one hand and grabbed her hair with the other.

Longarm took a step back. He knew he should try to get between the two women and put a stop to this . . . but his mama hadn't raised any fools back there in West-by-God Virginia. Interfering now would be a good way to get his own eyes scratched out.

Maureen drove a punch into Jessamine's belly, making her bend over in pain. That gave Maureen a chance to grab a handful of Jessamine's blonde hair and try to rip it out by the roots. Jessamine pulled harder in response, and both women squalled in pain and staggered back and forth across the aisle between the berths. All through the sleeping car, curtains were being pulled back now, and heads popped out through the openings as people tried to see what the hell all the commotion was.

A couple of female furies, that's what it was, Longarm

thought. Maureen and Jessamine let go of each other's hair and went to flailing away instead, throwing wild punches that missed half the time. Maureen was wearing a thin green robe that gaped open more and more as the belt around her waist began to slip. As she and Jessamine fought, she managed to hook a hand in the neckline of the blonde's filmy blue garment. With a ripping sound, the fragile fabric gave way all down the front. Jessamine screeched in outrage as most of her body was laid bare. One of her hands shot out, locked around Maureen's left breast, and twisted brutally. Maureen cried out in pain.

She lifted an elbow, cracking it under Jessamine's chin. Jessamine's head rocked back from the blow, and she was momentarily stunned. Maureen clubbed her hands together and swung them in a roundhouse blow that would have almost taken Jessamine's head off—if it had landed. As it was, Jessamine ducked backwards, causing Maureen's fists to miss her. Maureen stumbled, thrown off balance by the missed blow.

Jessamine tackled her around the waist. Both women went down, sprawling in the aisle in a tangle of bare arms and legs. Maureen's robe was more off than on by now. As the two women rolled over in their struggle, Longarm caught flashing glimpses of creamy thighs and triangles of fine-spun hair, one red, one dark blonde.

It was quite a show, all right, but he realized with a sigh that he couldn't allow it to go on any longer. One or both of the women was liable to get hurt if he didn't put a stop to this fracas. He took a step toward them and leaned over, saying loudly, "Here now, that's enough—"

He heard a crack and something plucked his hat off his head.

Instinctively, Longarm dove forward, both to protect the women and to make himself a smaller target. "Get down!" he bellowed, hoping the other passengers who were half-way out of their berths would duck back into cover. Both Maureen and Jessamine seemed to be stunned by his weight

130

descending on them so suddenly and unexpectedly, because they stopped thrashing around. Longarm tried to plant his left hand on the floor of the car but felt it land on soft female flesh instead. He pushed off anyway, hearing one of them go, "Ooof!", as he rolled over and grabbed for his gun.

Longarm caught a glimpse of a shadowy figure ducking back onto the platform at the front of the car. He threw a hurried shot in that direction but saw the slug chew splinters from the side of the door. Scrambling upright, he barked over his shoulder at Maureen and Jessamine, "Get in one of the berths!"

Without waiting to see if they followed his orders or not, he plunged toward the door, intent on not allowing the bushwhacker to get away this time.

Before he reached it, he blew out the lantern at this end of the car so that he wouldn't be silhouetted as he went through the door. Then he lunged out onto the platform, crouching low as he peered through the connecting walkway to the next car.

No one was there. The door of the next car was shut.

Where had the son of a bitch gone?

Longarm glanced up at the roof of the car. That was one answer. Not a particularly appealing one, he reflected grimly, but one that had to be checked out anyway.

He stepped across to the other platform and grabbed one of the iron bars bolted to the wall that formed a ladder to the top of the car. Climbing one-handed was awkward, but he wasn't about to holster his gun, not under such deadly circumstances.

Too bad his hat had already been blown off his head, he thought as he climbed. If he'd still had it, he might have put in on the barrel of his gun and poked it up above the level of the roof to see if it drew another shot. As it was, he had to risk his own skull. He edged high enough to see.

At the other end of the car, a dark shape was moving along the roof. Longarm had to concentrate a second to realize that the odd figure was actually down on all fours, crawling toward the front of the car. Clearly, the would-be killer wasn't comfortable up here.

Longarm, on the other hand, had had more than one shoot-out on top of a moving train. Staying upright was a matter of balance and good luck. He hauled himself over the edge of the roof and rolled into the center of it before he came up in a crouch and pointed his gun toward the dark figure at the other end of the car.

"Hold it!" he shouted.

The shape twisted around in a sudden, jerky motion that sent it slipping and sliding toward the edge of the car. Orange flame winked in the night from the muzzle of a gun. The shot went wild, so wild that Longarm didn't even hear the bullet passing him. He returned fire, triggering a couple of shots, but he aimed wide on purpose, trying to spook the bushwhacker into giving up. Whoever he was, Longarm had some questions to ask him.

A terrified yell came back to him. For a moment, the figure had stopped its slide toward the edge of the roof, but now it began to slip again. Still crouching, Longarm ran toward the front of the car. He saw arms flailing and slapping against the slick surface of the roof as the would-be killer tried frantically to stop himself again. This time, however, he failed, and with another scream, the man went plunging off the top of the train.

"Damn it!" Longarm grated. The bushwhacker was gone, vanished into the night. Longarm kept moving forward, since that was the closest way down off the roof now. He holstered the Colt and used both hands on the grab bars as he scrambled down to the platform.

Then he burst into the car and grabbed for the emergency cord. He heard the shrill blast of a whistle somewhere, then the squeal of brakes. The train lurched heavily, throwing Longarm off his feet. This was one of the passenger cars, and the mostly male passengers were jolted off the benches by the sudden stop. Angry shouts and questions filled the air as the train finally shuddered to a halt.

Longarm scrambled up, lunged out onto the platform,

and leaped to the ground on the same side of the tracks as the bushwhacker had fallen. He drew his gun again as he ran back the way the train had come.

Suddenly, a shape loomed up in front of him, and Longarm saw moonlight wink on the barrel of a gun. He almost fired, holding off at the last second when he spotted the shape of the cap on the man's head and recognized him as the conductor.

"Hold it, mister!" the conductor said. "Drop that gun!"

"I'm a U.S. deputy marshal," Longarm said quickly. "I'll show you my badge and my bonafides if I got to, but right now I'm looking for a gent who just fell off the roof of this car a ways back."

"Fell off—what the hell are you talking about?"

Longarm forced himself to keep a rein on his temper. "The fella tried to ambush me. I chased him up on top of the train, and he slipped and fell off. I got inside and pulled the emergency cord as quick as I could, so he's probably not more'n a few hundred yards back along the tracks."

"And you say you're a lawman?"

"That's right."

The conductor hesitated a second longer, then said, "I've got a bull's-eye lantern in the caboose. Let me get it, and we'll have a look along the tracks."

Running footsteps sounded, and as Longarm and the conductor were walking toward the caboose, the engineer and fireman joined them. "What in blazes is going on?" the engineer demanded.

The conductor jerked a thumb toward Longarm. "This gent is a federal lawman. He's looking for somebody who took a shot at him, then fell off the top of the train."

"Fell off?" echoed the engineer. "Why, that's the craziest thing—"

"I saw it happen," Longarm said. "And I'm hoping the hombre's still alive."

The engineer snorted. "Not likely. I was highballing along pretty good."

Longarm knew that. Chances were, the bushwhacker had

133

been killed by the fall off the moving train. But he had to be sure.

That took about five minutes. By that time, Longarm and his three companions had walked along the tracks, the conductor shining the beam of the bull's-eye lantern in front of them, until they located the broken, crumpled form of a man. Longarm knew as soon as he saw the odd angle of the head on the man's shoulders that he was dead.

With a curse, Longarm knelt beside the body, which was lying facedown. He felt for a pulse, knowing he wouldn't find one, then grasped the man's shoulder and rolled him over. Longarm hadn't recognized the man's clothes, and when the light washed over the man's face, frozen in a grimace of pain and fear, it wasn't familiar, either. Longarm had never seen him before.

"Well, hell!" Longarm said.

"Do you know him, Marshal?" asked the conductor.

"Nope, and that's what's got me mad. Why in Hades would a perfect stranger try to gun me?"

"You're a lawman. Maybe this fella had a grudge against you for something you did in the past," the fireman suggested.

Longarm had considered that very possibility earlier in the day, that the bushwhacker was just some outlaw or outlaw's kin who hankered to see him dead. Maybe that was the case. Longarm studied the man's face keenly. There was nothing unusual about it. It lacked the coarse, heavy features of a lot of desperadoes, however. In fact, the gent looked rather clean-cut. The only sign of a misspent past was a scar on his jaw where somebody had probably raked the point of a knife . . .

A frown etched itself into Longarm's forehead. The man who had tried to steal the Wild West Show's payroll from Kurt Schilling back in Kansas City had had a scar on his face, too. Maybe there was a whole ring of scar-faced outlaws on the loose, Longarm thought, then discarded the idea as being ludicrous, like something out of one of those yellow-backed dime novels that Schilling enjoyed.

He came to his feet. "Well, I won't be asking this gent any questions," he said. "We'd better put him back on the train so we can leave him with the undertaker in Hays."

"I'll have to report this incident to the local law, too," the conductor said.

"Report all you want to," Longarm told him. Turning away from the corpse, Longarm walked back toward the train.

What looked like at least half the passengers had gotten off and were milling around, trying to find out why the train had come to such a sudden stop out here in the middle of nowhere. As Longarm neared the group, several members of the Wild West Show saw him coming and hurried out to meet him. Colonel Pettigrew was in the lead, and he said worriedly, "I say, I say, son, what happened back there?"

"Somebody fell off the train," Longarm replied.

Maureen stepped forward. She had managed to wrap the robe around her again and tie the belt tightly. "The man who was shooting at you?" she asked.

Longarm would have just as soon kept the bushwhacking attempt quiet among the passengers, but it was too late for that. Too many people had witnessed it, anyway. He said, "That's right."

"You're not hurt, are you?" Maureen asked anxiously.

He shook his head. "Nope. Not a scratch." Which was more than Maureen could say. In the light that came from the windows of the nearest train car, he saw several scrapes on Maureen's face. They had been left behind by Jessamine Langley's fingernails, he knew.

Maureen came into his arms and hugged him. Longarm asked quietly, "How about you? You and Jessamine call a truce?"

"Don't talk about that . . . that hussy. I don't want to ever see her again."

That was going to be difficult, considering that they were in the same show. But Maureen would likely get over being so mad, Longarm told himself, once she realized that he wasn't really interested in Jessamine.

Kurt Schilling said, "Were you able to find the man's body, Marshal?"

Still holding one arm around Maureen, Longarm nodded. "Yep."

"Did you recognize him?"

"Never saw him before in my life. Don't know if he got on the train in Kansas City or boarded at one of the stops since then." Longarm glanced over his shoulder and saw the engineer and fireman approaching, carrying a grim, blanket-shrouded bundle. The conductor must have come back to the train and fetched the blanket, Longarm thought.

The conductor was in front of the other two trainmen. He shooed the passengers back into the cars, saying, "There's nothing to be alarmed about, folks. Just go back inside, and we'll get started on our way as soon as we can. Shouldn't be very long."

Grudgingly, the onlookers went, including the members of the colonel's troupe. Longarm walked with Maureen to the sleeping car. He paused to help her up to the high step onto the platform, since the portable steps that were usually set up were still inside the car. With one hand on her arm and the other on her hip, Longarm gave her a boost.

As he did so, he glanced along the train toward the engine. A couple of cars away, he saw a woman climbing to the platform there. She turned her head in his direction, then quickly pulled herself up and out of sight. Longarm had seen her face for only a fraction of a second, and that had been in dim, uncertain light.

But he recognized her anyway, and the knowledge of her presence on the train hit him like a fist slugging into his gut.

"Custis?" Maureen asked from the platform of the sleeping car. "Custis, what's wrong?"

Longarm gave a little shake of his head. "Nothing," he said as he took hold of the grab bar and stepped up to the

136

platform himself. "I reckon I'm just a mite spooked by everything that's happened tonight."

"I can understand why, nearly getting killed that way. And by a perfect stranger, too. That's really puzzling."

"Yeah," Longarm said. "Puzzling."

"Well, come with me, and I'll take your mind off it. Just because our plans were interrupted earlier doesn't mean we can't go on with them now."

"I reckon not," Longarm agreed.

But even as he went with Maureen, Longarm knew he wouldn't be able to give his full attention to what he was about to do. His mind was on another woman, the woman he had glimpsed getting onto the train a few moments earlier.

As far as he had known, Katherine Nash was on her way back to Washington and the Bureau of Indian Affairs by now.

What the hell was she doing on a train bound for Denver instead?

Chapter 14

Longarm was glad there were some things a fella could do strictly on instinct. Maureen didn't seem to notice how distracted he was while he was making love to her. She probably would have been pretty peeved if she'd known that he was thinking about another woman the whole time. And not about Jessamine Langley, either, which would have been the likely conclusion for Maureen to jump to.

No, Longarm was thinking about Katherine Nash.

By morning, he hadn't come up with any answers. Could be that the BIA had sent her on another assignment after she'd reported Longarm's findings about the so-called Princess Little Feather. That wasn't very likely, since the Bureau didn't really send its agents gallivanting around all over the country—preferring to keep them in Washington and use poor fellas such as U.S. deputy marshals to do their dirty work for them—but it was at least possible.

Longarm decided he would just find Katherine Nash and ask her. Sometimes the simplest, most direct methods were the best.

Unfortunately, Katherine didn't seem to be on the train anymore.

That was the conclusion Longarm came to after searching through all the cars while the train was stopped for breakfast in Hays, Kansas. Most of the passengers had gotten off to take advantage of the opportunity to eat breakfast in the Harvey House, which was adjacent to the depot. Longarm looked through the restaurant first, then went from car to car looking for Katherine. There was no sign of her.

Longarm stood on the platform of the last passenger car and fired up a cheroot after chewing on it in disgust for a moment. Katherine had given him the slip. That meant she had seen him the night before as she was getting back onto the train, and for some reason, she was afraid that he had recognized her. Why would that possibility bother her, unless she had something to hide? Why would she try to avoid him this morning?

Maybe the answer had something to do with men who had what looked like knife scars on their faces . . .

Longarm pondered on that for a few minutes, making some connections he couldn't prove yet and seeing the glimmering of a picture with several sections still shrouded in shadow. But the half-formed theory tied in with something he had noticed earlier. He just needed more information to fill in some of the gaps.

He didn't waste any more time looking through the train. Instead, he headed for the Harvey House, intent on a plate full of bacon and eggs and flapjacks. No point in starving himself just because folks kept trying to kill him, he told himself.

"Where were you, Custis?" Maureen asked him when he joined her at one of the tables in the restaurant.

"Oh, just stretching my legs. A fella gets a mite cramped up riding on a train."

Although how anyone lucky enough to share Maureen Mullaney's bed could ever get cramped up, he didn't know. A fella had to be pretty limber to keep up with Maureen.

"I went ahead and ordered some breakfast for you," she said. "I knew you'd be hungry, after you used so much energy last night."

Longarm grinned. "Much obliged. For everything."

"I'm the one who should be thanking you," Maureen practically purred.

Longarm might have enjoyed a few more minutes of suggestive banter with her, but right then a heavy hand fell on his shoulder and a man's rough voice said, "Marshal Long?"

Longarm stood up, shaking off the hand, and turned to see a man in late middle age with a salt-and-pepper soup-strainer mustache. He wore a town suit, a string tie, and a broad-brimmed black hat. His coat had a silver badge pinned to it.

"I'm Sheriff Cranston," the man went on. "The conductor from that train stopped over to the depot tells me you killed a man last night."

"Well, not exactly," Longarm said. "What killed him was falling off the train. We were swapping lead at the time, though."

"You claim this gent tried to perforate you?"

"That's right," Longarm nodded. "When his first shot missed and he figured I was going to shoot back, he climbed on top of one of the cars. That was his mistake. He slid right off."

Sheriff Cranston grunted. "Reckon it was pretty clear he died of a busted neck, all right. I took a look at the body down to the undertaker's. You got any idea why the fella wanted you dead?"

Longarm shook his head. "Nary a one. I don't suppose you recognized him?"

It was Cranston's turn to shake his head. "Nope. I stopped by my office on the way here and went through all my reward dodgers without finding him, too. As far as I can tell, the fella wasn't wanted anywhere."

That jibed with some of the conclusions Longarm had come to earlier. In fact, he would have been mighty surprised if the sheriff had recognized the dead bushwhacker.

"Well, Sheriff, you seem to know as much about this now as I do. Are you going to need me for the inquest?"

Cranston shrugged. "Reckon it'd be better if you could

stick around, but I know you got a train to catch. I'll have my deputy write up a statement real quick-like, and he can bring it over here for you to sign 'fore the train pulls out again."

Longarm nodded and said, "That sounds like it'll work."

Cranston tugged on the brim of his hat and nodded to Maureen. "Ma'am." He turned and left the restaurant.

Longarm's food had arrived while he was talking to the local lawman. He sat down and dug in with gusto, realizing just how hungry he was. Not many things affected his appetite for very long.

He chatted pleasantly with Maureen while he ate. There was no sign of Jessamine Langley in the Harvey House, so Longarm supposed she had remained on the train. Probably to hide a black eye or two, he thought with a grin. He wasn't accustomed to having a couple of pretty gals brawling over him, but it was nice when something like that happened now and then.

Sheriff Cranston's deputy showed up with the statement for Longarm to sign. After glancing over it to make sure it was accurate, he scrawled his moniker at the bottom of the page and said, "There you go, old son."

A few minutes later, the train's conductor entered the restaurant and announced, "Five minutes, folks. Train's leaving in five minutes."

The passengers hurried to finish up their meals and take care of any other business they needed to do, then headed for the train. Longarm linked arms with Maureen as they strolled toward the club car. He kept an eye out for Katherine Nash but didn't see her anywhere. She was doing a good job of hiding out, wherever she was.

This stopover was about halfway to Denver. The train would arrive in the Mile High City in the pre-dawn hours of the next morning. Longarm hoped the rest of the trip would pass without any trouble, but he didn't expect that to happen. Too much had gone on already. Somewhere out there were more people who wanted him dead; he was sure of that much, even though he didn't understand exactly *why* they wanted to see him pushing up daisies.

To his surprise, the day passed quietly. The train clicked along the rails with nothing to slow it down, and Longarm passed a pleasant day in the club car, sipping Maryland rye and talking to Maureen, Colonel Pettigrew, Asa Wilburn, and several other members of the Wild West Show. Kurt Schilling wasn't there, and Pettigrew explained that the bookkeeper was indisposed. "Reckon he ain't used to ridin' the train yet," Pettigrew said. "His innards are all riled up."

Longarm could understand that. The train's rocking and swaying motion wasn't as bad as being on a boat, but it bothered some people after a while.

That evening, Longarm and Maureen were able to retire to Maureen's berth without any of the interruptions of the previous night. Once they'd gotten their clothes off, Longarm stretched out on his back in the bunk while Maureen straddled him. She lowered herself onto his erect shaft, the massive pole of male flesh filling and stretching her femininity until she gasped. Longarm cupped her buttocks as she rocked back and forth gently and slowly. Their mouths met in a hungry kiss.

Going at it like that, it took a long, pleasurable while before their climaxes swept over them. Longarm tightened his grip on her hips as he spurted his seed into her, then instead of withdrawing, he stayed where he was, buried inside her. His shaft softened some, but after an interval of nuzzling and kissing and stroking, he grew hard again. "Ready to go some more?" he asked in a whisper.

Maureen replied by grinding her groin against his.

Eventually, they both fell asleep, but not before Longarm had come several times. Maureen was satiated, not to mention filled to the brim. Sometime during the night his organ slipped out of her, but when he awoke, long after midnight, she was still cradled on the broad, hairy bed of his chest, sleeping soundly.

With the curtains pulled, it was pitch-dark inside the berth. Even if Longarm had been able to fish his watch out of his clothes, he wouldn't have been able to read it. He knew, though, that the train hadn't reached Denver because it was still moving. He suspected it was around four in the morning, which meant there was another hour or so to go before the train would pull into the depot.

As he lay there, half-dozing, Longarm heard a stealthy tread in the aisle between the berths. There was nothing particularly unusual about that. Anyone moving around in a sleeping car in the middle of the night would normally be quiet about it. That was just common courtesy.

So many odd—and dangerous—things had happened in the past few days, however, that Longarm was instantly keyed up, just in case the soft footsteps meant more trouble. Maureen must have sensed his muscles stiffening, because she raised her head a little and murmured drowsily, "Again?"

Slap-and-tickle wasn't what Longarm had in mind, however. Instead, as he heard the rustle of fabric, he suddenly tightened his arms around Maureen and rolled to the side, away from the curtains.

The berth wasn't very wide. Maureen let out a surprised exclamation as she was shoved hard against the wall by Longarm's action. Longarm felt the curtains brush against his back as they were swept aside. Close by, someone grunted with effort, and Longarm felt the bunk's mattress jerk. He was lying on his right side, so that put his left arm on top. He lashed out behind him with it, striking blindly.

His fist smacked into something. He heard another grunt, this one of surprise and pain. He let go of Maureen and rolled back the other way, toward the curtains. Cold steel sliced into his side, tracing a shallow, fiery line across his flesh. Longarm ignored the pain as best he could and pitched out of the berth, tackling the man who had just cut him with a knife.

It was as dark in the aisle as it was inside the berth. Longarm couldn't see a damned thing, and he knew the lurker must have blown out both lanterns before skulking along the aisle to Maureen's berth. Expecting to feel the knife blade biting into his flesh again at any second, Longarm struggled with the man as they both lay in the aisle.

"Custis?" Maureen asked from the darkness in a quavery voice.

Longarm didn't waste any breath answering her. He had his hands full with the desperate, shadow-cloaked struggle in which he found himself. His left hand, fumbling in the darkness, found his attacker's wrist and closed around it. Assuming the fella was right-handed, that would be his knife hand, Longarm thought, so he went with the odds and held on tightly. At the same time, his right hand, questing blindly, encountered the man's throat. Longarm's fingers clamped shut like a vise.

All he had to do now was hang on until the erstwhile assassin passed out from lack of air, he thought. That might have worked if something hadn't crashed into the side of his head, stunning him and knocking him to the side. As he toppled off his attacker, the man tore free from Longarm's grip and lunged upward. A foot smashed into Longarm's ribs, adding to the waves of pain that were coursing through him.

Vaguely, he heard the other man panting for air and knew that his chokehold had almost worked. Longarm rolled, hoping to avoid another kick. He heard a rustle of clothing and felt something sweep through the air near him. He figured he had just avoided another slash of the attacker's knife. He kicked up and out, hoping to connect with something.

His heel buried itself in something soft and yielding, and he heard a hiss of pained, indrawn breath. Hoping that he'd just kicked the bastard in the balls, Longarm rolled again, this time to put more distance between him and the other man. He came up on one knee.

A faint grayness seeped into the car through the windows of the doors on each end. That predawn light served to show Longarm a shadowy shape several feet away from him, now that his eyes were finally adjusting. The figure

144

was unsteady on its feet, and Longarm knew he had done some damage.

The fight had taken place in near silence, so the occupants of the other berths hadn't been disturbed. Maureen knew something bad was going on, though, and when Longarm heard the familiar metallic click of a gun's hammer being drawn back, he knew she had gotten her hands on either his Colt or one of her own guns.

"Don't move," she ordered tersely. "I'll shoot if you do. Custis, where are you?"

The idea of Maureen pointing a gun blindly out here into the aisle made a cold chill go along Longarm's spine. She'd be just as likely to shoot him as she would the intruder unless he spoke up. Quickly, he said, "Over here, Maureen."

Then he dropped to his knees, knowing his voice would give the killer something to aim at. He sensed as much as heard something pass close beside his ear and then a clatter sounded behind him. The man had thrown the knife in a last-ditch effort to carry out the intended killing.

"I warned you!" Maureen cried.

Longarm lunged up, lashing out with an arm as he snapped, "No!" He hit Maureen's arm just as the gun in her hand cracked. A thud told him that the slug had gone harmlessly into the ceiling. There were too many innocent bystanders in this car for anybody to start shooting, no matter how good their intentions were.

And what with the shot and all the yelling, the aisle would probably be crowded in a few seconds with people wanting to know what all the commotion was.

Longarm heard rapid footsteps and knew the assassin was fleeing. For a second, Longarm considered going after him, then remembered that he was naked and unarmed. Besides, people were already starting to spill out of their bunks. "What is it?" a woman called. "Was that a shot?"

Grating a curse, Longarm reached into Maureen's berth. "Gimme my pants," he said. He found them himself and pulled them on, then reached into the berth again and located the little packet of lucifers he always carried in one of his vest pockets. He snapped one of the matches alight with an iron-hard thumbnail, well aware that by doing so he was once again making himself a target. He felt fairly confident the killer was long gone by now, though, and anyway, the man hadn't had a gun or he would have used it when his attempt to kill Longarm quietly had gone awry.

"Oh, my God!" Maureen exclaimed when the yellow circle of light from the lucifer spread around Longarm. "Custis, you're hurt!"

Longarm looked down and saw the trickle of blood from the shallow gash in his side. It could have been a lot worse. If he hadn't reacted instinctively when he did, the knife would have plunged right into Maureen's back. The would-be assassin would have killed the wrong person, but the fact that she wasn't the real target wouldn't have made Maureen any less dead.

Those thoughts flashed through Longarm's brain, but he kept them to himself as he said, "It's just a scratch." Maureen might figure out for herself just how close she had come to dying, but Longarm wasn't going to tell her and spook her that much more.

Longarm looked up and down the aisle. Several women had poked their heads out from their berths, and a few had even ventured out in their nightclothes. A couple of well-fed, middle-aged men were in evidence, too, both of them wearing nightshirts. Longarm pegged them as prosperous businessmen traveling with their wives. Nobody he saw looked like a killer. He was certain the person he'd grappled with had been a man, and the attacker hadn't been wearing nightclothes, either. That meant he'd managed to get out of the car, just as Longarm had suspected.

"It's all right, folks," he assured the passengers. "Just a scuffle with a gent who was probably a sneak thief. I don't reckon he'll be coming back."

Longarm knew that was a lie. The knife-wielder wasn't a sneak thief at all. His only purpose in skulking into the sleeping car had been to kill Longarm.

And he'd come too damned close to succeeding, Longarm thought.

The lucifer burned down. Longarm shook it out and dropped it on the floor of the car. He reached for his clothes as the other passengers began to retreat into their berths.

Maureen slipped out of the bunk. She had a strip of cloth in her hand, probably torn from the hem of one of her petticoats. Grudgingly, Longarm allowed her to tie the makeshift bandage around his torso.

"You should have a doctor look at that wound," she said.

"I'll go to the club car and get a little whiskey to pour on it," he said. "That'll do the trick. Trust me, Maureen, I've patched up more'n my share of these nicks."

"I'll just bet you have. You forget, Custis, I've seen the scars all over you. You must attract bullets and knives like a magnet."

"I seem to attract trouble, right enough."

And even though the train was nearing Denver, the trouble wasn't going to stop, he thought. Somebody—maybe more than one somebody—wasn't going to be satisfied until he was dead.

And it was damned well about time that he found out why.

Chapter 15

The conductor had been notified about the ruckus in the sleeping car. By the time he got there, Longarm was fully dressed and waiting for him.

"Trouble again, Marshal?" the conductor asked with a frown.

Longarm nodded. "It surely does seem to follow me around, don't it?"

"I'm told there was a thief here in the car, and you struggled with him."

Longarm inclined his head toward the platform at the end of the car. "Let's go talk about it out there."

The conductor hesitated, then nodded. He followed Longarm onto the platform.

Dawn was approaching even faster now. The sky in the east was a rosy pink. Up ahead to the west, the mountains of the Front Range were now in sight, looming dark against the vestiges of night. Longarm saw a sprawl of twinkling lights that he knew to be Denver. From this angle, the city appeared to be nestled at the foot of the peaks, but Longarm knew that was deceptive. Denver was actually a good many miles from the mountains.

"All right, Marshal, let's have it," the conductor demanded. "What's going on here?"

Longarm took a deep breath of the cool early morning air. "That fella I was waltzing with inside wasn't trying to rob anybody," he said. "He was trying to kill me."

"Another would-be murderer?" the conductor asked skeptically. "I know lawmen make a lot of enemies, but you can't seem to go twenty-four hours without somebody trying to kill you."

Longarm shrugged. "It may seem sort of odd, but that's the way it is. I've got a knife gash on my side that stings like blazes to prove it."

"You're wounded?" the conductor asked anxiously.

"Nothing to worry about," Longarm replied with a casual wave of his hand. "The fella almost missed me clean with his pigsticker."

"Do you have any idea who he was?"

Longarm had some ideas, all right: he wouldn't have been at all surprised if the gent turned out to have a scar on his face somewhere. That seemed to be a common thread running through this whole mess.

But he didn't say that to the conductor. Instead, he said, "Let me ask you a question. Is there a passenger on board named Katherine Nash? Good-looking woman about thirty, built slender, with ash-blonde hair? You can tell by looking at her she's a lady."

"That sounds like Miss Wilson."

"Wilson, eh? Boarded at Kansas City?"

"As a matter of fact, yes. You don't mean to tell me that she has something to do with this, do you?"

That was exactly what Longarm thought. He was convinced that Miss Wilson was actually Katherine Nash using a phony name.

"You happen to know where she is now?"

"Why, I suppose she's sitting up in one of the cars. She didn't reserve a sleeping compartment."

No, she wouldn't have, thought Longarm. She would have wanted to be free to move around, so that she could stay out of his way and avoid being seen by him. It had been pure bad luck for her that he had caught a glimpse of her the night before last.

"Have you seen her since we stopped in Hays yesterday morning?"

"Yes, I have. I spoke to her yesterday evening, in fact."

So Katherine was still on the train. She must have had a hell of a time ducking him while he was searching for her, Longarm told himself. That she had succeeded in doing so told him how important it was to her that he not be allowed to confront her.

"All right. How much longer to Denver?"

The conductor took out his watch and checked it. "We're on schedule. We'll pull in at the station in twenty-one minutes."

"Thanks." Longarm started to turn away.

The conductor stopped him with a hand on his arm. "I still don't know what's going on here, Marshal, but I'll respect your wishes and not pry any further. I would like to know, though, if there's anything I can do to help."

"Can't think of a thing, old son, but I appreciate the offer." A smile tugged at Longarm's mouth. "I reckon you'll just be glad to get me off your train."

"No offense, Marshal . . . but you're right. I think once you're gone, the trouble will be, too."

The same thought had crossed Longarm's mind. In fact, he was sure of it.

The sun still wasn't up when the train pulled into Denver. Longarm had told a puzzled Maureen that he would see her later. He wasn't particularly worried that anything else would go wrong where the Wild West Show was concerned. The danger to Maureen and nearly everyone else in the show had come about because *he* was with them, not the other way around as Longarm had thought at first.

He swung down from one of the cars onto the depot platform even before the train had completely stopped moving. Quickly, he strode across the platform and ducked into a little alcove where he could watch the passengers disembarking from the train without being noticed himself. He stayed back in the shadows of the unlit alcove.

The platform was a beehive of activity as the members of the Wild West Show, along with all the other passengers who'd been bound for Denver, left the train and tended to their baggage. Longarm watched as Colonel Pettigrew supervised the unloading. Ben Price, Tom Beaumont, and the other wranglers led the horses down ramps from the freight cars that had been converted into rolling stables. Jessamine Langley wore a hat with a veil over her face, hiding the marks of her battle with Maureen just as Longarm had suspected. Asa Wilburn and Kurt Schilling strolled together across the platform, an unlikely duo but one that seemed to be quite common. The bookkeeper had attached himself to the lanky frontiersman, and Wilburn, glad to have an audience for his stories of the old days, didn't seem to mind.

It took the better part of an hour to get all the troupe's gear off the train and loaded onto wagons that would carry it to the hotel that would serve as the headquarters of the Wild West Show during its stay in Denver. The sun was up by the time the caravan set off for the downtown area.

Longarm didn't venture out of his hiding place until they had gone. He had watched for Katherine Nash, too, but he hadn't seen her get off the train. More than likely, she had been afraid that he would be watching, so she had slipped off the other side and stolen away into the early morning, intent on the mysterious errand that had brought her here to Denver.

Longarm felt a little better now that he was back here in his old stomping grounds. He might not know everything that was going on, but he had an inkling of how to get some more answers. He planned to stop by his rented room on the other side of Cherry Creek, then go to Billy Vail's house and roust his boss out of bed. He smiled at that thought. Billy was always complaining about how Longarm came in to work late; the chief marshal was about to get an unusually early visit from his wayward deputy.

151

It would take Vail's clout, Longarm thought, to get the information he wanted. Once Longarm had explained a few things, Vail could start burning up the telegraph wires between here and Washington. Longarm was confident that Billy would raise hell about what was going on and wouldn't stop yelling until he got some straight answers.

People were starting to be out and about on the streets. Longarm walked quickly to his rooming house, let himself in, and went upstairs. His room was small, since he didn't do much more than sleep there. As he paused in front of his door, he glanced down. The matchstick he'd placed between the door and jamb nearly a week earlier was still there. He twisted his key in the lock, turned the knob, and stepped inside.

A cold ring of metal pressed to the side of his neck.

But it wasn't any colder than the female voice that said quietly, "Step inside, Marshal, and shut the door. Gently. No need to wake up the other tenants."

Longarm's jaw tightened. He pure-dee hated to have somebody get the drop on him, even someone as talented as Katherine Nash had to be. She must have spotted the matchstick and replaced it so that he wouldn't have any warning she was waiting inside the room. He said tautly, "Now, Miss Nash, we both know you ain't going to shoot me. How can I keep on being a stalking horse for you if I'm dead?"

He heard Katherine Nash take a deep breath. "You're right, I can't shoot you." The gun barrel went away from Longarm's neck. He started to relax a little, then Katherine said, "But I can do this."

Longarm tried to get out of the way of the blow, but he was too late. Katherine was quick, he had to give her credit for that. The butt of the little pistol slammed into the back of Longarm's head, just above his neck, and skyrockets went off in his brain.

Those were the last lights he saw before darkness closed in and claimed him.

• • •

Some time later, Longarm stirred and groaned. The black tide receded as consciousness came back to him.

"Good," Katherine Nash said. "You're awake."

Longarm blinked his eyes open and raised his head. He squinted at the window and judged by the amount and quality of the light coming through the curtains that he hadn't been unconscious for very long, probably no more than a couple of minutes. But as he tried to move his arms and found them trapped behind him, he realized that had been long enough for Katherine to snap a pair of handcuffs around his wrists.

"Get these damned bracelets off of me," he growled. "I thought we were on the same side."

"We are," Katherine assured him. "But I've heard many stories about how impulsive and headstrong you are, Marshal. I wanted to make sure you would listen to me before you went charging off and ruined everything."

She was sitting on the edge of his bed, her knees primly together. Longarm was lying in the floor on his left side, about four feet from her. Just to look at Katherine, you'd never know she was such a scheming, cold-blooded bitch, he thought.

"I'll listen to you," he said. "But I still want these cuffs off. They're damned uncomfortable."

She frowned hesitantly. "Do I have your word that you'll hear me out? That you won't leave until you fully understand the situation?"

"Hell, understanding the situation is what I've been after right from the first!" With an effort, Longarm reined in his temper. "But it wasn't important that I understand then, was it? All that mattered was that I kept luring those scar-faced killers out into the open by poking around the Wild West Show. You and your bosses didn't decide to let me in on it until I spotted you on the train."

Katherine's expertly plucked eyebrows lifted slightly in surprise. "If you've figured out that much, I suppose you already know quite a bit."

"Not enough." Longarm squirmed a little and lifted the

wrists cuffed behind his back. "Now, about these brace-lets—"

"Your word," Katherine reminded him.

He glared at her for a second, then sighed. "All right. I give you my word I'll hear you out."

"Good." She stood up and took a small key from her bag. "I know quite a bit about you, Marshal, and I've been told that you're a man who doesn't lie." She bent over him, the delicate scent of her perfume filling his nostrils in the otherwise stuffy room. The lock on the handcuffs clicked, and they fell away from Longarm's wrist.

His hand shot out, clamped around one of her ankles, and pulled.

With a startled cry, Katherine fell backward. She landed on the bed and started to bounce. She couldn't because Longarm landed on her.

"You . . . you bastard!" she gasped as he grabbed both of her wrists in one hand and pinned her arms above her head. "You gave me your word!"

"I'm listening," Longarm said. His lips were pulled back from his teeth in an expression that was half-grin, half-grimace. With his free hand, he plucked up the bag she had dropped on the bed when she fell. He upended it and dumped out the pistol she had held against his neck earlier, then used to knock him out. It was a puny little thing. Longarm had expected better of her. He said as much as he flicked open the cylinder and dumped the shells, then tossed the gun into the far corner of the room, adding, "A pistol like that ain't accurate if you're more'n five feet from what you're trying to hit."

Through gritted teeth, Katherine said, "I'm seldom more than that far away from a man I want to shoot."

"No," said Longarm, "I reckon you ain't."

The implication of that made her spit and sputter angrily. Longarm stood up and kept his grip on her wrists, hauling her upright with him. He lowered her arms so that he was holding her wrists between their bodies. Her eyes were still flashing fire. Her hat had come off, and some of the ash-blonde curls had come loose from their elaborate arrangement so that they hung enticingly around her face. Longarm wouldn't have minded kissing her right then, if he hadn't been afraid that she would try to gnaw his lip off.

"All right," he said. "I'll talk first, and you'll tell me whether I'm right or not. You don't work for the Bureau of Indian Affairs at all, do you?"

"Of course I do. I just . . . work for another government agency, too."

"The Secret Service?"

Her lips set stubbornly.

"I'll take that for a yes," Longarm said dryly. "I know how stubborn you folks are about admitting things like that. So you really work for the Secret Service and your job with the BIA is just a false front."

"You're telling this story," Katherine gritted.

"That's right, I am. You came to my hotel room in Kansas City and spun that yarn about Chief Lame Bear and his poor disappearing daughter just so I'd have an excuse to visit that Wild West Show. I never heard of no Pawnee chief named Lame Bear. Is he real?"

"Of course he is. And his daughter was lost during a battle some years ago. It *could* have been feasible that the woman calling herself Princess Little Feather was indeed the chief's daughter."

"Yeah, if she wasn't really a redheaded Irish gal named Maureen. I'll bet you knew *that*, too, before you ever came to see me."

Katherine shrugged. "It was a convenient story, and I didn't think anyone would challenge it."

"How'd you know I wouldn't just pay one visit to the Wild West Show and never go back?" Longarm's eyes widened in horror. "Hell, you weren't to blame for the stampede that killed Alf Culpepper, were you? You didn't do that to draw me in?"

"Of course not!" Katherine exclaimed. "But we knew a lot of mysterious things had been happening since the show left the East, and we were hoping you'd be intrigued enough to investigate."

"Even though it was completely out of my jurisdiction?"

She smiled, but it wasn't a pleasant expression. "You have a reputation, Marshal Long, for sticking your nose in where it doesn't belong whenever something catches your interest, despite any rules and regulations."

Longarm bit back a curse. He had played right into their scheming hands, doing everything they expected him to do just like a good little puppet. He didn't know whether to feel mad as hell or sick at his stomach. The answer, he decided, would depend on her response to his next question. "Did Billy Vail know about this?" he asked quietly. If his boss and old friend had set him up like this . . .

"No," Katherine said. "Marshal Vail wasn't informed of our plans. My superiors back in Washington said, and I quote, 'That stubborn old mossback would never stand for it.' "

Knowing that Billy hadn't been involved in the deception made Longarm feel a little better. He knew as well that once this was all over, Vail would raise one hell of a stink about one of his deputies being used this way. Longarm let go of Katherine's wrists, giving her a little shove at the same time that made her sit down on the bed again. He stepped back and rubbed a hand wearily over his face. He hated politics and the way it sometimes stuck its ugly head into what should have been a simple job of keeping the peace and bringing lawbreakers to justice.

"Your bosses were right about Billy," he said. "If they'd told him what they were planning, he'd have lit into them like a gila monster." Longarm drew a deep breath. "So, once you had me staked out like a judas goat, you figured those boys who are after Schilling would try to eliminate me first."

Again, Katherine looked surprised. "You know that Schilling is involved?"

Longarm snorted and said, "Hell, I've known that for a couple of days, ever since I got a whiff of one of those fancy Egyptian quirlies he smokes. I haven't quite figured out, though, why he wanted to burn down that arena in Kansas City. If he's trying to hide out in the Wild West Show, why would he want to ruin it?"

Katherine shook her head. "I don't know for sure, but I suspect the Prussians made another try for him that night, and he started the fire as a distraction so that he could get away from them. He was desperate, you know, and perhaps not thinking straight."

Longarm considered the theory and nodded slowly. "Could be," he said. "They sure tried for me that night. One of 'em with a rifle nearly ventilated me a couple of times. Good thing they don't handle rifles as well as they do sabers." He scraped a thumbnail along his jaw. "Schilling must not have gotten one of those dueling scars at Heidelberg like the others. But they were old pards of his anyway, weren't they?"

"My God," Katherine said, staring at him. "We underestimated you, Marshal."

"Folks've been known to," Longarm said.

"Perhaps we should have just assigned you to the job of protecting Schilling from the start, instead of staging such an elaborate deception."

Longarm shrugged. "I've gotten rid of two of the assassins for you, the one who fell off the train and the gent who shot it out with Schilling in The Cattlemen's Hotel. There never was any holdup attempt, was there?"

Katherine shook her head. "No, that was strictly another assassination attempt. Schilling was foolish enough to be caught alone that morning, instead of staying with Asa Wilburn or some of the other members of the Wild West Show."

"Wilburn ain't working for you, is he?"

"Not at all. Our theory is that Schilling simply attached himself to Wilburn thinking that such a man would be able to come to his aid in case of trouble."

That jibed with Longarm's own thinking. No wonder Schilling had stuck so close to the old frontiersman. Despite his age, Wilburn was likely hell on wheels in a fight, and Schilling had recognized that.

"Does Schilling know that the Secret Service is keeping an eye on him?"

Again Katherine shook her head. "Not that we're aware of. When he left Washington with the information he'd gathered, we believe he had no idea we had discovered he was a spy. Then, when we received word from an agent of ours inside Bismarck's government that Schilling had double-crossed his own country and planned to sell his information to the highest bidder, we knew we had to make sure nothing happened to him. We knew, as well, that the Prussians would come after him."

Longarm's head was starting to spin. He had been involved in this sort of international intrigue a few times before in his career, in cases where there was no black or white but only shades of gray, and he hated it.

He tried to get all his ducks in a row by saying, "All right. Schilling was a Prussian spy and got his hands on some sort of important information in Washington. But instead of sending it back to his bosses in Europe, he took off on his own. Bismarck sent a bunch of killers after him to get rid of him and get the information. Your bosses knew about all this, so they got you to send me to the Wild West Show in hopes that I'd pull at least some of the assassins into the open and maybe even get rid of them for you. Is that about the size of it?"

"You're remarkably astute, Marshal."

"Where's Schilling headed? He's not just running blind."

"No, we agree on that point," Katherine said. "The show's ultimate destination is San Francisco, and that's where we think Schilling wants to go. We suspect he has some sort of meeting set up there with someone who wants to buy the information from him."

"Who might that be?"

"I honestly don't know," Katherine said.

Exasperated, Longarm asked, "Why don't you just step

in and arrest Schilling? He can't pass along any information if he's locked up behind bars."

Katherine didn't answer.

After a moment, Longarm's eyes narrowed. "Damn it! You don't want to grab Schilling until after you find out who wants to buy the information from him."

"The world is changing, Marshal," Katherine said stiffly. "It's to our advantage to know which countries are really our friends and which ones are our enemies."

"Maybe so," Longarm said. He thought about something else. "What about that stampede?"

"I have no idea," Katherine declared. "We had nothing to do with it, and I don't see how the Prussians could have, either." She paused, then added, "I'm surprised you recognized those men for what they were. They were trying to pass for Americans, you know."

Longarm shrugged. "A dueling scar looks pretty much like any other scar a fella would pick up in a knife fight in a cantina or somewhere, I reckon. But I knew Schilling had mentioned the University of Heidelberg, and I recollected reading something about how they particularly like to fight duels over there. Seemed pretty far-fetched to think that somebody would travel all the way from Europe to go gunning for a bookkeeper in a second-rate Wild West Show, but the more I pondered on it, the more likely it seemed. That got me started thinking about Schilling, and I knew he'd had something to do with that fire because I smelled those cigarettes of his just as it was starting. None of it really added up, but it was just too much to ignore."

Katherine stood up and said, "I congratulate you, Marshal. Now you know the whole story. Can I count on you to continue working with us until this case is brought to a successful conclusion?"

"There's just one more thing . . ." Longarm said slowly.

"What is it?"

"That's what I want to know." Longarm's voice was grim. "Just what is it Schilling knows that's come damned close to getting both him and me killed?"

Chapter 16

Katherine Nash shook her head. "I can't tell you."

"Damn it—" Longarm began with a growl.

"No, I mean I really can't tell you," Katherine insisted. "My superiors deemed that was something that was unnecessary for me to know. All I was told was that it was information vital to the interests of the country."

Longarm scowled. "Probably the names and addresses of all the politicians' back-street gals in Washington."

"It really doesn't matter," Katherine said. "What's important is that Schilling lives to complete his rendezvous in San Francisco. Can we count on you to help us, Marshal?"

"You want me to go all the way to California with the Wild West Show?"

Katherine nodded. "That might be best."

Longarm suppressed the impulse to groan in dismay. When this was all over, he vowed, he was going to ask Billy Vail to send him after some nice simple gang of outlaws. Chasing down a bunch of owlhoots and shooting it out with them sounded a hell of a lot more appealing than trying to follow the shadowy mazes of the game being played by Katherine, Schilling, the Prussian assassins, and some politicians in Washington and Berlin.

He blew his breath out in a sigh. "All right," he said. "Whatever you need."

"Excellent. When I wired my superiors from Hays after you saw me getting back on the train, I suggested that it would be better at this point to take you into our confidence. I'm glad you've proven me right, Marshal."

Katherine's hat was on the floor where it had fallen when Longarm jerked her feet out from under her. He bent over, picked it up, and brushed it off before handing it to her. "Schilling ought to be all right for the day," he said. "He'll be around Wilburn and the others while they're setting up for tonight's show. So what I want to do is get some sleep between now and then."

"That sounds reasonable." Katherine tucked the stray strands of hair back into place before settling the hat on her head. As Longarm watched her doing that, her gestures simple yet somehow intimate, he was struck by a pang of desire. He would sleep even better, he thought, if he was to bed this slender, ash-blonde beauty first.

But that was probably a bad idea, he told himself. As much as he might enjoy the challenge of warming Katherine up, he'd be worried all the time that she might be planning to double-cross him again. She was a hell of a kisser, he remembered, but romping wasn't everything.

"I'll be at the show tonight," he said, a little more harshly than he intended. "I reckon you'll be around?"

"You won't see me, but—"

"Yeah, I know."

Katherine started toward the door, then stopped and looked back at him. "We all do our duty to our country in different ways, Marshal," she said quietly.

Longarm couldn't argue with that. He just stood there impassively as she left the room, then he got undressed and threw himself down on the bed.

Sleep was a while in coming.

Longarm got up in the early afternoon, washed up, put on fresh clothes, and went down the street to the Chinaman's hash house for a late breakfast. He didn't go to the Federal Building, knowing that if he went to Billy Vail's office he would have a hell of a time explaining everything to the chief marshal. Longarm wasn't totally sure he had all the story straight himself. Despite what Katherine had said, there could have been things she hadn't told him. Truth was a relative thing where most folks connected with the government were concerned.

Instead, he holed up in his room during the afternoon with an ample supply of cheroots, a pint of rye, and a couple of recent editions of the *Police Gazette*. He sipped from the pint only occasionally, since he wanted to have a clear head tonight.

Katherine had been right about one thing: The Secret Service should have told him the truth from the start. He would have had no trouble finding an excuse to stay with the Wild West Show so that he could bodyguard Schilling without the renegade spy even being aware of what was going on. If they'd done that, Longarm would have been on the alert and might not have come so close to getting killed. But he supposed doing things on the up-and-up went against the grain for folks who were used to such labyrinthine plotting, like Katherine's bosses.

Come to think of it, Longarm reminded himself, he was still pretty curious about the stampede that had claimed Alf Culpepper's life. Instinct told him it hadn't been an accident. If it wasn't, somebody had committed murder and gotten away with it so far, and that galled Longarm.

Maybe by the time the show reached San Francisco, he'd have that one figured out, too.

Colonel Pettigrew's troupe was booked into the Denver Municipal Arena for their performances. Longarm went back to the Chinaman's for supper, then headed for the arena as the sun disappeared behind the Front Range and dusk began to settle over the city. The gas streetlights came on, casting their yellow glow. Longarm saw quite a few fliers advertising the Wild West Show tacked up on walls or leaning in the front windows of businesses. Pettigrew's advance men had done their job, letting the paying customers who were hungry for entertainment know that a show was coming to town. As he neared the arena, he saw quite a few people headed toward the large building on the edge of the downtown area.

People were laughing and talking, and families were holding hands, looking forward to an evening of merriment. Longarm watched their faces closely, looking for any men who sported unusual scars. He didn't see anyone who looked out of place, but that didn't mean anything. The Prussian killers could still be out there somewhere, waiting for a chance to strike. During the performance, everyone in the troupe had something to do. Kurt Schilling's job was to count the money taken in for tickets. Unfortunately, that was a solitary task. If the assassins tried to strike at him, it would likely be during the performance, Longarm reasoned.

The closer the show got to San Francisco, the greater the danger to Schilling would be. Evidently, his former partners in espionage couldn't afford to let him get away with the information he had somehow gotten his hands on.

Longarm stood in line with the other customers waiting to buy tickets for the show. When he reached the window, the burly ticket-seller he remembered from Kansas City was there dispensing ducats. The man looked up and saw Longarm, and his eyes widened in surprise. "Hey, I remember you," he said.

"Keep it under your hat," Longarm advised as he laid some coins on the counter.

"But you're a—"

Longarm gave the man a hard look, shutting him up.

The ticket-seller's hand deftly swept the coins into the money drawer, and he tore a paper ticket off a roll to hand to Longarm. "There you go, sir," he said. "Enjoy the show."

"I plan to," Longarm lied. He didn't expect the evening to turn out enjoyable at all. He just hoped he would have a chance to steal some time with Maureen over the next few weeks as the Wild West Show made its way to San Francisco.

He walked into the arena with the rest of the crowd. The building was set up similarly to the one in Kansas City, with grandstands rising around a central, dirt-floored ring. The arena had been built for livestock shows and fairs, but in the future it would probably be used more and more for rodeos and performances like Colonel Pettigrew's show.

Longarm strolled all the way around the grandstand, smoking a cheroot as he went. If the Prussians were already here, he wanted them to get a good look at them. He had an itchy feeling in the middle of his back, as if there were a target painted on it. After he had made a circuit of the stands, he went down a hallway into the part of the big building where the dressing rooms and the offices were. Somewhere back here, he knew, was where Kurt Schilling would spend his evening.

A door opened in front of him, and Maureen stepped out into the corridor. She stopped short as she turned toward him. "Custis!" she exclaimed. "I didn't know if you were coming tonight or not."

"Couldn't keep me away with a team of wild horses," Longarm said with a grin. He ran his gaze appreciatively up and down Maureen's trim form. She was dressed in her Princess Little Feather costume again, and she had gotten another raven's-wing-black wig to replace the one lost in the fire in Kansas City. He had to admit, in that getup and with her usual peaches-and-cream complexion covered with makeup, she did look pretty much like a Pawnee princess. If her cheekbones had been higher, she would have been a dead ringer for one.

"Are you going to watch the performance tonight?" she asked as she came closer to him.

Longarm hesitated. Before he'd found out what the case was really all about, he would have said yes. Now, however, he knew that Kurt Schilling was the focal point of the whole mess, and he felt like he ought to stick closer to the bookkeeper/spy. "I'll try to see your part anyway," he told Maureen, deliberately avoiding a firm commitment.

She came up on her toes and brushed a kiss across his lips. "I'll be looking for you in the audience," she said.

"No need for that. You just concentrate on what you're shooting at."

"Always."

With a cheery wave, she headed toward the arena. Longarm went on down the hall toward the offices.

Colonel Pettigrew came out of one of them, trailed by Schilling. Longarm kept his face carefully impassive, not wanting Schilling to realize that his true identity was known to the big lawman.

Pettigrew greeted Longarm with a broad smile. "I say, I say, son, I didn't know you were goin' to be here tonight. Denver's your home, ain't it?"

"As much as anywhere is, I reckon," Longarm said. "But I suppose I've gotten used to being around you folks, Colonel. Besides, Cherokee Hank could get up to some more mischief."

"Aw, he's clear back in Kansas City, won't be comin' thisaway for another three or four days."

"That doesn't mean somebody working for him couldn't try to sabotage your show again," Longarm pointed out.

Pettigrew's broad forehead creased in a frown. "You know, you're right, son. We ain't out o' the woods yet, are we?"

"Maybe not." Longarm had decided he would play to Pettigrew's suspicion of Henry Trenton. That was the best way to explain his continued presence around the Wild West Show.

Schilling spoke up, saying, "Well, I for one appreciate your presence, Marshal. I hope having you around will stave off any evildoers."

"You and me both," Longarm agreed.

Pettigrew clapped Schilling on the shoulder. "Well, I got to get goin'. See you later, Kurt. Enjoy the show, Marshal."

"I intend to," Longarm said. He waited until Pettigrew had waddled away up the corridor before turning to Schilling and asking, "I reckon you'll be back here counting the money during the performance?"

"That *is* the bookkeeper's job," Schilling said, smiling mildly.

"Whereabouts is your counting room?"

"That office we just left," Schilling said, turning halfway around to point to the door.

"Anybody besides you standing guard over that money?"

"Marshal, do you suspect me of some plan to steal the show's proceeds?"

Longarm shook his head. "Nope, but I ain't forgot about what happened in Kansas City. Somebody else could decide to try to grab the loot again."

"I see what you mean." Schilling opened his coat a little to reveal the butt of the small pistol holstered under his arm. "But anyone who tries will get an unpleasant surprise, *nicht wahr?*"

"You did seem to be pretty handy with that," Longarm admitted. "Good enough to keep that gent from holding you up, anyway." He paused, then went on as if just thinking of it, "Say, I recollect reading something once about how fellas at the University of Heidelberg like to fight duels with swords. Is that right?"

Schilling tensed slightly, but Longarm's deliberately guileless bearing must have convinced him that the question was just innocent curiosity. "There is a dueling society, yes."

"They do it for fun, not because they want to kill the other fella?"

"Fencing is a sport, Marshal Long. But at Heidelberg, it is taken quite seriously. A dueling scar is regarded as something of a badge of honor, especially among the young men of the Prussian aristocracy."

"You ever fight any duels?"

Schilling smiled. "I was an instructor, a simple mathematician, not a student at the university. And certainly not a member of the aristocracy."

Longarm nodded and said, "I just got to wondering about that. I reckon them Prussian aristocrats think of those dueling scars like some young Sioux warriors think of the

166

scars they get from the sun dance and rituals like that."

"Exactly," Schilling agreed, his interest perking up a little. "And just as you have read of the Heidelberg duelists, I have read of the sun dance. I would like to see it someday."

"I don't know," Longarm said slowly. "The Sioux—all the tribes, for that matter—are sort of touchy about outsiders watching their sacred rituals."

"But surely, a man such as yourself has witnessed such things."

Schilling's keen interest in the American West seemed genuine, Longarm decided. Well, there was no reason why a spy couldn't be interested in other things besides espionage. Longarm shrugged and admitted, "I've seen the sun dance, as well as the ghost dance and the snake dance and a bunch of others."

"We must sit down and talk someday, Marshal. I have been picking the brain of poor Mr. Wilburn about the history and customs of your American frontier ever since I joined the troupe. I fear that he is getting tired of my questions."

Longarm chuckled. "I wouldn't worry about that. Most old fossickers like Asa are glad to have somebody to listen to their stories. I reckon I'll be the same way, happen I ever get to be that age."

"Why would you not reach that age?"

"I ain't in the most peaceful line of work," Longarm said dryly. "Most star-packers don't die in bed."

"Ah. Of course. I hope you do, Marshal. I hope you have a long and fulfilling life."

"I reckon we'll find out, if we wait long enough," Longarm said with a grin.

"Well," Schilling said, "I must be on about my business." Music sounded from the center of the arena. "The grand parade is starting, and you are missing it."

"I've seen it before. How do you get the money to count?"

"Dolph will bring it back here once he closes the ticket

window, when the show is about half over."

"What do you do until then?"

Schilling frowned a little, and Longarm wondered if he had pushed the questions a mite too far. "I work on bringing the books up to date," said Schilling.

Longarm nodded. "I'll let you get to it, then." He turned and started back along the hall.

A glance over his shoulder showed him Schilling retreating into the office. Longarm stopped, swung around, and stepped over to a door. He wasn't sure what was on the other side of it, but if the room was empty, he could wait in there with the door open a crack and keep an eye on the counting room that way. He grasped the knob, twisted it, and swung the door open.

"Oh, my God!" a woman gasped.

Longarm froze. He was looking into a storage room. There was a small table inside it, along with plenty of clutter, and sitting on the edge of the table was Jessamine Langley. She was wearing her riding outfit, or at least some of it. The short, spangled skirt lay on the floor. In front of Jessamine, standing between her widespread legs with his trousers down around his ankles as he drove his stiff organ into her, was Tom Beaumont. The wrangler looked back over his shoulder at Longarm and snarled a curse. "Get the hell out of here, damn you!"

Muttering an apology, Longarm started to back out of the doorway so the two of them could get on with what they were doing. He had only taken a single step when the muzzle of a gun pressed painfully against the small of his back.

"I say, I say, don't move, son. I'd sure as hell hate to have to blow a hole in you right here and now."

Chapter 17

Sheer surprise kept Longarm from moving or speaking for a moment. The same didn't hold true for Tom Beaumont, who bent down to grab his trousers and haul them up around his waist. As he turned away from Jessamine, she scrambled down off the table and hurriedly picked up her skirt.

Beaumont took a step toward the doorway and said angrily, "Now who in hell's out there? Can't anybody get any privacy around here, damn it?"

"I reckon not, Tom," Colonel Pettigrew said. He shoved Longarm hard in the back, forcing him into the storage room.

"Colonel?" Beaumont exclaimed. Music from the arena drifted into the room through the open door. "What's going on? What are you doing in here, Colonel? You're missing the grand parade."

"Aw, hell, the rest of the troupe's done it plenty of times. They can manage without me. I told Maureen to lead it this time. She was right honored." Pettigrew took the gun away from Longarm's back. "Move over there with them other two, Marshal."

Longarm thought about trying to turn quickly and knock the gun out of Pettigrew's hand. That probably wouldn't

169

get him anything except a bullet in the spine, he decided. The wheels of his brain were clicking over rapidly. Pettigrew had to have a damned good reason for what he was doing. Longarm could think of only one such reason that might appeal to the colonel.

Money.

Longarm turned slowly, keeping his hands in plain sight so that Pettigrew wouldn't get trigger happy. "How much are they paying you, Colonel?" he asked.

"That's none of your business, son. It'll be enough to get me out o' this hole I dug for myself, though. The show can go on."

"It'll be blood money, you know that," Longarm said. "They'll kill Schilling. But they're liable to torture him first, if he doesn't give them what they want."

Jessamine said, "I . . . I don't know what any of this is about. I just want to go do my part of the show."

"Sorry, darlin'," Pettigrew drawled. "I reckon I'll have to find a new trick rider after a while."

"Colonel, what do you mean?" she asked nervously. "I've always done everything you asked me to. Even when you wanted me to . . . to pleasure you."

Pettigrew nodded solemnly. "And you was damned good at it, too. I'll miss that even more'n the fancy ridin'."

Beaumont turned to Jessamine and growled, "Is there anybody in this show you *haven't* rutted with?"

"Stop it, Tom," she quavered. "Please, don't be mean to me. Not now."

Beaumont gestured toward Pettigrew. "Don't you understand? He's going to kill us!"

"Not until after the Prussians have Schilling," said Longarm.

"I don't know anything about that," Beaumont snapped. "Let Jessamine and me go, Colonel, and we'll keep our mouths shut."

Pettigrew shook his head again. "Sorry, Tom, can't do it. Can't take the risk."

"It won't be a risk," Beaumont said desperately. "I'll

170

give you something to hold over my head, just like we'll have something to hold over yours. I started the stampede that killed Alf Culpepper."

Longarm glanced over at Beaumont. He'd heard a heap of confessions in his years as a lawman, some genuine and some nothing but a pack of lies. As he looked at Beaumont, he sensed that the wrangler was telling the truth.

"You did, Tom?" said Pettigrew. "I say, I say, why, boy?"

"Because of Jessamine, of course," Beaumont replied bitterly. "I thought Ben Price would be the one to get trampled. I stole some flash powder from that photographer who took pictures of the troupe a couple of days earlier, and when I set it off, it spooked the horses so bad they stampeded. That part worked just like I planned."

Jessamine was staring in horror at Beaumont now. "You . . . you did that?" she said.

The wrangler's lip curled in a snarl. "You never would have left Price on your own. You were having too good a time playing him and me against each other."

Longarm was convinced that Beaumont was telling the truth about the stampede. But it wasn't going to do them any good because Pettigrew still had a pistol leveled at them, and the expression in the showman's eyes was merciless.

"I'm sorry to hear about that, Tom," Pettigrew said, "but it don't change nothin'. I can't afford to let you folks live."

Longarm asked, "How are you going to explain our deaths?"

"Shouldn't be that awful hard," Pettigrew said with a shrug. "Ol' Tom here come bustin' in on you and Jessamine, Marshal, and when he saw you humpin' her, he just sort o' went crazy and started shootin'. He managed to kill her and put a bullet in you 'fore you were able to down him. Then both of you up and died. Damned shame, if you ask me. But won't nobody question it too much, 'cause everybody connected with the show knows what sort o' gal Jessamine is."

171

"You old son of a bitch!" she practically spat at him.

The colonel looked sad. "Now, now. No call to be like that. We ought to try to remember all the good times we had, here in this last few minutes we'll be spendin' together."

Several sets of footsteps sounded in the hall. Longarm peered past Pettigrew through the open door and saw four men hustling Kurt Schilling along the corridor. Schilling's hands were tied, and a gag was in his mouth. His eyes were wide with terror as they rolled momentarily toward Longarm.

One of Schilling's captors, a tall, lean man with a scarred cheek, paused in the doorway and said in a heavily accented voice, "Ve vill leaff now, Colonel."

Pettigrew waved his free hand toward the doorway without looking away from the three people he was holding at gunpoint. "You go on ahead, boys." He patted the breast pocket of his buckskin jacket. "I've got my payoff right here, and it's plenty to put the show right back on its feet."

The Prussians forced Schilling on down the hall. Clearly, they intended to slip out of the arena and take Schilling someplace they could dispose of him safely after they had gotten the information they wanted out of him. Longarm wondered if Katherine Nash was anywhere around, and if she was, would she spot the kidnapping attempt and be able to stop it? Right now, it didn't look like Longarm was going to be a damn bit of good to her.

But he had never expected Colonel Pettigrew to turn traitor like this.

"I told Maureen to go ahead with her Princess Little Feather act first tonight, since she was leadin' the entrance," Pettigrew went on. "That was a stroke o' good luck. I didn't know I was goin' to find anybody back here 'cept Kurt. Now that I have, once Maureen commences to shootin', won't nobody hear another few shots comin' from here."

"You bastard," Beaumont grated.

"Well, now, I'm mighty sorry you feel that way, son."

Longarm took a deep breath and asked, "Mind if I smoke a cheroot first?"

Pettigrew frowned. "I wouldn't deny a feller his last wish. But make it fast, son. We ain't got much more time."

That was sure as hell the truth, Longarm thought as he reached inside his vest pocket and drew out the little two-shot derringer that was welded to the other end of his watch chain. His hand concealed most of the weapon. He had a cheroot between his fingers, too, but as it came clear of his pocket, he dropped it.

Pettigrew's eyes naturally followed the falling cigar, and when they did, Longarm snapped the derringer out and pulled the trigger. The weapon went off with a wicked little crack, and Pettigrew's head jerked back as a small, black-rimmed hole appeared in his forehead. His finger clenched involuntarily on the trigger of the pistol as he died. The gun blasted, and Beaumont grunted and took a step backward, doubling over. His hands went to his belly, clutching at himself as blood began to well through his fingers. Jessamine screamed.

Colonel Pettigrew's knees folded up, and he pitched forward on his face. Jessamine kept screaming as Beaumont crumpled to the floor of the storage room, too.

Longarm felt a brief twinge of pity for her, suddenly being surrounded by death like that. But he didn't have time to comfort her now. He jumped over Pettigrew's bulky corpse and raced out of the storage room, turning to follow Schilling and his Prussian captors.

They were no longer in sight. Longarm grimaced as he tried to figure out which way they had gone. He had been in the Denver Municipal Arena on several occasions in the past, but he didn't know the place all that well, especially this part that was off-limits to the general public.

As he hurried down the corridor and turned a corner, he heard gunshots coming from the central part of the building. That would be Maureen launching into her trick-shooting act, he thought. He could tell that was what it was because of the evenly spaced nature of the reports. A real

173

gunfight sounded a lot more confused than that.

Longarm went around another corner and found himself in the dirt-floored runway between the central arena and the corral area. A glance toward the gates told him most, if not all, of the wranglers were up there watching the show, ready to lend a hand if anything went wrong. At this point in the performance, the corral area would be almost deserted. That was the easiest way out of the building, he decided. He turned toward the corrals and broke into a run.

He heard the sounds of a struggle as he reached the mazelike fences of the corrals. He couldn't see Schilling and the Prussians. Quickly, Longarm climbed onto one of the fences so that he would have a better view of the area.

As soon as he did, somebody took a shot at him.

The slug whizzed past his head. Longarm spotted the Prussians then, still trying to force Schilling out of the building. Through the open doors, Longarm caught a glimpse of a waiting wagon. He brought up his Colt and fired, driving a couple of bullets between the group of struggling men and the doorway to turn them back. At that moment, the frantically struggling Schilling finally managed to break free. He drove his bound hands into the belly of one of the Prussians and tore out of the man's grip. Turning, he sprinted back toward the center of the building.

Longarm dropped from the fence as another shot came his way. This one knocked his hat off his head but left him otherwise untouched. He fired through the openings between the slats of the fences, the kind of trick shot that even someone like Maureen might not be able to make. Longarm's slug found its target, though, spinning one of the Prussians off his feet.

The other three took off after Schilling, pausing just long enough to throw a couple of shots in Longarm's direction. Keeping his head down, he began circling the pens in an attempt to intercept the assassins. He came out at the end of the runway just as the Prussians reached it as well. Terror had given Schilling wings, and he was almost at the other end, where the big gates let out into the arena.

One of the men rapped a command in German to the other two, and they went after Schilling. The leader, who wore a long coat, blocked Longarm's path. This was the man who had spoken to Pettigrew earlier, the one with the scar on his cheek that almost pulled his left eye closed. He smiled as he reached under his coat. Longarm heard the rattle of metal on metal, and then the Prussian had a sword with a long, thin blade in his hand. He moved it back and forth slowly in front of him as he grinned at Longarm.

"Are you a man of honor?" he asked in a sneering tone.

"Sorry, old son, right now I ain't got time to be," Longarm said. Then he shot the Prussian, drilling him neatly through the right thigh. The man went down with a scream, dropping the saber and clamping his hands to his bleeding leg. Longarm stepped past him and reversed the Colt long enough to slam the butt against his head, knocking him cold. Then Longarm went after the other two Prussians and Schilling.

The renegade spy had reached the knot of wranglers. With the gag still in his mouth, he couldn't ask for help, but Ben Price saw him and grabbed him, saying, "Kurt! What the hell!" He reached up and pulled the gag down.

"Stop them!" Schilling screamed. "They want to kill me!"

Longarm heard that, saw the wranglers turn toward the Prussians. Clearly, their orders had said for them to kill Schilling whether they were able to recover the information or not, because they opened fire. Price stumbled back with a bullet in his side, and two more of the wranglers fell. Schilling twisted away, pushed the gate open, and ran out into the arena, where Maureen was still performing.

The audience didn't know a damned thing about what was going on, Longarm realized. They had to have heard the extra shots, but to them it was all part of the show. They whooped and hollered as Schilling stumbled out onto the hard-packed dirt of the arena.

"Out of the way!" Longarm bellowed at the wranglers who were crowding around their fallen pards. He bulled his way through them and out into the arena himself, hot on the heels of the foreign assassins.

Up ahead, in the center of the arena, a startled Princess Little Feather turned toward the men who were interrupting her performance. Even at this distance, Longarm saw the surprise on her face as she spotted him.

"Schilling!" Longarm shouted. "Get down!"

He didn't know if Schilling obeyed his order or if the bookkeeper just tripped. But Schilling suddenly pitched forward, facedown in the dirt. One of the Prussians spun toward Longarm, while the other one drew a bead on Schilling.

Five guns roared almost as one. Longarm fired a fraction of a second before the Prussian who was aiming at him. The man was driven back by Longarm's slug slamming into his chest. The Prussian's shot plowed harmlessly into the dirt near Longarm's feet.

At the same time, Maureen fired both the pistols in her hands. The slugs ripped into the remaining assassin, making him twitch grotesquely as he got off a single shot of his own. Like that of his companion, his bullet went into the ground. He fell over backward, landing with his arms and legs spread.

The audience roared and applauded, and if any of them noticed the blood seeping into the dirt floor of the arena, they must have thought it was fake.

With his Colt still in his hand, Longarm strode forward and kicked away the fallen weapons before he checked on the two Prussians. Both of them were dead. Maureen had been firing live ammunition during this part of her show, and Longarm was grateful for that. Blanks wouldn't have done much good this time around.

"C-Custis?" she asked as she approached him, raising her voice to be heard over the noise of the audience.

He put his free hand out and rested it on her shoulder. "Are you all right, Maureen?" he asked.

"I . . . I'm fine." She looked down at the man she had

shot. Longarm felt a shudder go through her body. "I killed that man."

"And I'm mighty glad you did, otherwise he'd have likely killed you. And I *know* he'd have killed Schilling here." Longarm bent over and grasped Schilling's arm. He hauled the smaller man to his feet. Schilling was trembling like a leaf in a high wind.

"M-Marshal Long?" he said. "Those . . . those men were insane! I cannot thank you enough for saving me. They . . . they seemed to think I was someone else—"

"Ain't no use in pretending anymore," Longarm said grimly. "Not after all this." *Not after more than half a dozen people had died.*

"Really, Marshal, I—I do not know what you mean—"

"I'm sure somebody back in Washington'll be glad to explain it to you." Shrill whistles drew Longarm's attention, and he turned to see more than a score of uniformed Denver police officers entering the arena. The audience got the idea then that something was really wrong, and the level of noise in the arena, already loud, went up a notch or two. It was damned near Pandemonium, in fact, Longarm thought.

"Well," said Longarm, "I reckon this show's over."

"I don't much care for being kept in the dark like that." Billy Vail's voice was soft, but Longarm recognized the anger that lurked in it. He had heard that tone often enough himself over the years.

"I'm sorry, Marshal," Katherine Nash said. "The decision was made in Washington, at the very highest levels."

"Well, on *this* level, we play it straight with our fellow peace officers," Vail said.

Katherine shrugged daintily, indicating that it was out of her hands, and anyway, what was done was done.

Longarm, who was sitting in the red leather chair next to Katherine's in front of the chief marshal's desk, cocked his right ankle on his left knee and leaned back. Billy wasn't likely to start foaming at the mouth, not with a lady in the room, and for once he didn't have a damned thing to yell at Longarm about. All through this case, Longarm had followed orders.

Right up until the time he had spilled the whole thing to Schilling, anyway. Katherine was still a mite peeved about that. The government wouldn't be finding out who Schilling had planned to sell his stolen information to after all. That is, not unless he decided to tell them himself after he'd been behind bars for a while, serving a long sentence for spying.

Katherine got to her feet. "If there's nothing else, Marshal, I'll be going. I have a train to catch. I'm due back in Washington."

Vail and Longarm stood, too. "Good-bye, Miss Nash," Vail said. He didn't sound like he would miss her very much.

Longarm had mixed emotions about that matter. He still wouldn't have minded seeing if there was a real flesh-and-blood woman under Katherine's cool facade. But he figured that wasn't likely to happen, and besides, he was supposed to meet Maureen in a little while.

Katherine turned to him. "Good-bye, Marshal Long."

"You still ain't going to tell us what Schilling knew that was so all-fired important, are you?"

"I still don't know," she said. "I doubt if I ever will."

Longarm shook his head. He never knew whether to believe her or not. "Good-bye, Katherine," he said.

When she had left the office, Billy Vail sat down with a sigh and said, "Good Lord, what a mess!"

"Yep," Longarm agreed. "But I reckon it could've been worse. Ben Price is going to recover from that bullet wound, things worked out halfway right for the government, and I found out who started the stampede that helped rope me in."

Vail reached for Longarm's report, which the rangy deputy had turned in earlier. "Just how many cases did you have going on at the same time, Custis?" He ticked them off on his fingers. "That whole spy business, Beaumont starting the stampede because of that trick rider gal, and maybe some sabotage by a rival Wild West Show. You were never able to establish whether this Cherokee Hank Trenton had anything to do with Pettigrew's bad luck or not, were you?"

Longarm took out a cheroot. "My bet would be that he didn't, but no, I didn't find out for sure. And like Miss Nash said, I don't really expect to. But it don't matter. Colonel Pettigrew's show is over and done with, just like the colonel himself."

Vail tossed the report down and said, "Pettigrew dead, Beaumont dead, all those damned Prussians except one dead, and him and Schilling behind bars. You cut a wide swath, don't you?"

"Hell, Billy, don't blame it on me!" Longarm scratched a lucifer to life and lit the cheroot, ignoring the glare Vail sent his way when he shook out the match and dropped it on the floor. "I was pretty much of an innocent bystander in this one."

"Innocent bystander!" Vail snorted. "Go on, Custis, get out of here. Take a few days off."

Longarm was glad to oblige. On his way out of the office, he glanced at the banjo clock on the wall. Five o'clock. He still had plenty of time to meet Maureen for supper.

When he reached the hotel, he found her waiting for him in an armchair in the lobby. She stood up and kissed him. Longarm drew her tighter against him, despite the fact that they were in public. Maureen was lovely in a dark blue dress, and Longarm felt himself responding to her as he always did.

Maybe they ought to go up to her room first and then have a late supper, he thought.

A hand fell on his shoulder, causing him to break the kiss and turn rather sharply. He found Asa Wilburn standing there in buckskins, a grin on his weathered, craggy face.

"How'd you youngsters like to go have supper with an old man?" Wilburn asked. " 'Course, I reckon you'd have to pay, Marshal, since it turned out the colonel had even less money than we all thought he did. Lord knows if we'll ever get the wages we had comin' to us."

"Poor Colonel Pettigrew," Maureen said. "He was really desperate."

Longarm squinted at her. "Poor Colonel Pettigrew?" he repeated. "He was just about to kill me and Beaumont and Miss Langley in cold blood!"

"Yes, but he wouldn't have been driven to that unless he really loved the Wild West Show," Maureen said. "Still, I don't suppose I should pity him."

"Nope," said Wilburn, "not when there's old-timers like me that a pretty young gal like you can pity."

Longarm slipped an arm around Maureen's waist. "I don't reckon we'll have supper with you, Asa. I don't think I trust you around Maureen."

"Story o' my life," Wilburn said, shaking his head sadly. "Oh, well. Leastways, with the show breakin' up, I got a good excuse to go back to the mountains, maybe have me another hunt. Might go back to Abilene and find my ol' pard Nestor, see if he wants to go with me."

Longarm stuck out his hand. "Good luck, Asa. I hope you find some frontier still left."

"So do I," Wilburn said as he shook hands with Longarm. "So do I."

When the old frontiersman was gone, Longarm turned back to Maureen and said, "You know, I was thinking we might sort of postpone supper for a while and go upstairs . . ."

"That might be a good idea," she said with a smile, "providing that we can . . ." She came up on her toes, leaned close to his ear, and whispered a few suggestions.

A grin broke out on Longarm's face. "Yep, I reckon we can do that," he said. "At least a few times!"